"Martha Jane Orlando has skillfully created an Aesopian world where magic and morals collide, resulting in an inspirational read. *A Trip, a Tryst and a Terror* is beautifully written, heartfelt and engaging."

— Leah Griffith, author,
Cosette's Tribe

A Trip, a Tryst and a Terror takes you to a wonderful place where Southern history, real time drama, mystery, and magic come together to change lives. Regardless of your age or background, *A Trip, a Tryst and a Terror* will transport you into the world of Davy, and hold you there, making you hungry for more."

— Mimi Moseley, author,
Arm Around Shoulder/Hand Over Mouth

A Trip, a Tryst and a Terror

THE GLADE SERIES | BOOK 1

LITTLE CREEK BOOKS
A division of Jan-Carol Publishing, Inc.
Johnson City, TN

LITTLE CREEK BOOKS
A division of Jan-Carol Publishing, Inc.

A TRIP, A TRYST AND A TERROR
THE GLADE SERIES | BOOK 1

Martha Jane Orlando

Published November 2012
All rights reserved
Copyright © Martha Jane Orlando

ISBN: 978-1-939289-03-2
Library of Congress Control Number: 2012920139

You may contact the publisher:
Jan-Carol Publishing, Inc.
PO Box 701
Johnson City, TN 37605
E-mail: publisher@jancarolpublishing.com
www.jancarolpublishing.com

INTRODUCTION

Lynne Watts, author of
The Call and *Wyatt, the Wonder Dog* (series)

Ten-year-old Davy Murray just knows that he is about to experience the worst summer of his entire life. A remote farmhouse in the Nantahala Mountains of North Carolina, no electronics, a stepdad he can't stand, and a pesky sister who gets on his last nerve are just a few of the minor inconveniences he will have to put up with on the family vacation his mom and step-dad have planned. It will take something this side of miraculous to change Davy's angry, hostile attitude, and transform a family divided into a family united.

Written against the backdrop of an antebellum home deep in the Nantahalas, Martha Jane Orlando writes with insight, warmth and humor as she chronicles the Murray/Hunter family vacation. Blended families and their vacations can be a challenge in the best of circumstances, but when there is an age-old family dispute, an eccentric and mysterious grandfather, and a clever squirrel named Grey to stir the pot, this quiet, relaxing vacation takes on some very unexpected and dangerous turns. In her first novel, Orlando proves herself a masterful storyteller who understands and affirms the power of family to endure despite great hardship and loss.

ACKNOWLEDGMENTS

I have never been alone on this journey of writing *A Trip, a Tryst and a Terror*, and seeing it through to publication. The support, the love and the encouragement of so many along the way mean the world to me. It is with a humble heart, I now give thanks—

To God, who blessed me with a talent for writing, gave me the inspiration for this story, and who never left my side as I wrote it.

To my parents, Bill and Nancy Murdy, and my mother-in-law, Miriam Orlando, for their confidence and belief both in me and my novel. Your love and support has been invaluable.

To my children, Daniel, Sarah Jane, Giovanni and Nicco, who always cheered me on and never doubted that this mom was destined to be a writer.

To my editor and sister-in-Christ, Diana Erbe, whose meticulous editing of this manuscript is surpassed only by her Godly insights, wisdom, and advice she shared with me throughout this entire process.

To my publisher, Janie Jessee, for believing in my work and for taking on this unknown author in faith. Her guidance, encouragement, and patience with me could, undoubtedly, make her a candidate for sainthood.

To the staff at Jan-Carol Publishing, Inc.—what an amazing job you did with the copy and design for *A Trip, a Tryst and a Terror*!

To authors Leah Griffith, Mimi Moseley, Lynne Watts and Glynn Young who graciously took time out of their busy schedules to read my novel and write such inspiring reviews for this book.

To my Facebook and blogging families—you have stood by me through this entire journey, supporting me and lifting my spirits when I needed it most. You made me realize how true this saying is: You can never have too many friends.

And, last, but definitely not least, to my husband and best friend, Danny Orlando, whose unconditional love for me and unwavering faith in my writing brings indescribable joy to my life. Darling, you have been and always will be the wind beneath my wings. I love you!

*A Trip, a Tryst and a Terror is dedicated
to loving stepfathers everywhere,
but, especially to Danny, John and Joseph.*

CHAPTER 1
ROAD TRIP

Davy slouched in the backseat of his mother's car as it hummed along the highway. Any other time, he would have vied with his sister, Anna, for the front seat privilege, but not today. *Not any other day, either*, his thoughts stormed, *not after Mom and that jerk of a stepdad ruined my summer.* He crossed his arms defiantly and glared icily at the back of his mother's blonde head. It was bobbing ever so slightly as she carried on a giddy conversation with Anna about all the fun they could look forward to when they arrived at Grandpa Will's house. He had heard enough of that story in the previous days as Mom and Jim, his stepfather, tried to convince him that this summer would be the most splendid ever.

Davy closed his eyes and replayed the scene which took place at the apartment several days earlier . . .

"There is so much to do there, Davy," his mother gushed. "You'll have acres of woods to explore, a stream and a lake to play in . . ."

"Or fish in," Jim, an outdoor enthusiast whose interests were not shared by Davy, interjected.

"There's a vegetable garden to tend to," Mom continued, "chickens to feed, and Grandpa's dog, Maggie, to play with.

1

Maggie needs someone like you to love her now that Grandpa's passed on."

Davy was almost converted by this last tidbit of information. He had always wanted a dog, but Mom insisted that apartments were not suitable places for them. They needed plenty of space to roam and play. The temptation of having a dog flickered briefly but was then replaced with a greater concern.

"But, there aren't any other kids there to play with," Davy argued.

"You don't know that," said Jim. "Sure, the place is pretty remote, but there are neighbors within a couple of miles. I'm sure we can round up a boy your age somewhere."

"No way," Davy stated vehemently. "Any kid living in the boonies is probably a redneck. I bet he wouldn't know the first thing about *Halo*.

The *Halo* games were Davy's absolute favorites to play. He always pretended he was a real soldier in combat, fighting for freedom, just as his dad had fought in Iraq. But, unlike the soldiers in the video games who could magically resurrect after being felled or return to the screen unscathed when a new game was initiated, his dad's sacrifice was an ultimate finality. He died a hero, protecting the lives of the men in his battalion. As the years passed, that hero status grew exponentially in Davy's eyes. This glorified perception prevented him from seeing in Jim, a military man himself who now taught JROTC at Winston High, any redeeming qualities. As far as Davy was concerned, he was a loser and his mom was an even a bigger loser, not to mention a traitor to dad's memory, because she was dumb enough to marry him. To top it all off, if it weren't for Jim's grandfather dying and leaving to him the farm in his will, none of this summer nightmare would even be happening. *There has to be a way out of this,* thought Davy.

"Mom, he whined, "why can't I stay with Uncle Frank and Aunt Jane for the summer?" Uncle Frank was his dad's brother.

He and Aunt Jane had a large house, a swimming pool, two dogs, three cats, and no kids. Whenever Davy or Anna visited with them, they reveled in being spoiled rotten. Uncle Frank had even let Davy have ice cream for breakfast during his last visit.

"Now, Davy," Mom chided, "it's one thing to stay with them for a week, but for the entire summer? That would be an absolute imposition. Besides, they are planning to travel to Europe this July."

"I could go with them!"

"Davy, be realistic; they've dreamed of taking this vacation for years, not to mention how much they saved for it, and I can tell you right now, as much as they love you, they couldn't afford to take you along."

"Well, then, let me stay at their house. I can take care of the dogs and cats for them."

Jim determinedly entered the fray.

"Davy, you're all of 10-years-old. I don't think housesitting is any kind of option for a kid your age, or anyone under 18, for that matter."

Davy glowered at him. Jim either didn't notice or chose to ignore the deadly daggers launched in his direction.

"Besides, your mom tells me you've always wanted to learn to shoot a gun. Grandpa Will was the one who taught me how to shoot a BB gun at the farm when I was about your age. We went through lots of tin cans, I can tell you. What do you say we buy you your very own BB gun as an early birthday present? I'd love nothing better than to teach you how to shoot. It'd be fun for both of us."

Davy's birthday was July 1st, a whole month away. Memories of previous years' celebrations flashed instantaneously before his eyes: pool parties (hosted by Uncle Frank and Aunt Jane, of course), movies, putt-putt golf, sleepovers where no one actually went to sleep but competed in video games until dawn. These all had one component in common: friends! This birthday, there would be no friends. The thought of spending his eleventh birthday in the company of a whiney sister, a mom who didn't care how he felt, and a step-father who rated one rung lower than pond scum was too much for Davy to bear.

"It won't be fun for me!" he shouted at Jim. "Nothing about this summer will be any fun for me! Do you hear me? *NOTHING!*"

He shook with an uncontrollable rage. Tears, unfamiliar visitors, knocked at the door of Davy's eyes.

"Calm down, buddy," Jim said in a soothing voice. Mom's voice seemed to have been shocked out of her.

"I'm NOT your buddy! I never want to be your buddy! You're a stupid jerk!"

Mom's voice made a miraculous recovery.

"Davy! How dare you call anyone such awful names, especially an adult and especially Jim? Apologize this minute!"

"NO!"

"David James Murray! NOW!"

"NO! You've both ruined my whole summer and you don't care. You're the ones that should be apologizing to ME! I hate you, both of you! I HATE you!"

At this last venomous attack, Davy's voice attained a piercing shriek that reverberated throughout the apartment and breached the paper-thin walls.

Nosy Mrs. Grant who lived next door surprised Mom several hours later with a book entitled *Raising Boys: A Parent's Survival Manual.* Her weak and all too transparent excuse for the gift? It was a going away present. Davy had left his room to which he had been confined indefinitely after his tirade and could vacate only to use the bathroom. When he heard Mrs. Grant's grating voice, he ducked behind the bathroom door, leaving it slightly ajar so he could eavesdrop without being noticed.

"More like a 'get lost' gift," Mom grumbled to Jim after Mrs. Grant's departure.

"Don't take it to heart, Kate," Jim said. "Bringing up kids has to be the hardest job out there, and you had to do so much of it without John's help. As far as I'm concerned, you've done good."

"Well," Mom corrected, aware that Jim knew better, but he knew that she was unable to control her compulsion to correct everyone's grammar, the natural fall-out from being a high school English teacher. The gesture was intended to diffuse her tension. It was at Winston High Mom and Jim had met two years ago. Even though he was only in fifth grade, Davy already dreaded the day he would attend Winston with not one, but two parents on the faculty. Correction: one parent, one jerk.

"I just don't understand what's gotten into Davy lately, honey," Mom lamented. "He was always such a compliant, easy-going child, polite and cooperative. I never imagined he would take the news of our vacation so poorly. I am certainly disappointed in him for being so rude to you."

"My skin's pretty thick," Jim assured her. "You have to remember we've only been married for two months, and it can take longer than two years for kids to adjust to a stepparent. Some kids never make the emotional connection."

You better believe I'm one of them, Davy thought spitefully.

"Look," Jim continued, "I've been realistic about this from the beginning. I know how Davy idolizes his father and that's how it should be. I just hope I can help him understand I'm not trying to fill those shoes."

Yeah, right, don't think I don't know what you're doing, Davy seethed.

Mom sighed heavily.

"Yes, I know," she said. "It's just that Davy needs a strong male role model in his life, whether he knows it or not. Frank has been great for a stop-gap, but he's too lenient. He spoils Davy and Anna shamefully every time they visit."

And, what's wrong with that?

"And, here you are, yet he seems to make every effort to avoid you. It's strange that he seemed okay with you while we were dating, but now, oh, I don't know, it's just all so frustrating and confusing."

Davy could hear her tears being choked back. For a moment, he felt sorry for his mother and the urge to run to her with a hug of comfort overwhelmed him. Impulsively, he abandoned his hideout and raced the few hall strides it took to reach the kitchen. He was too late. There was his mom, cradled in Jim's embrace. He was whispering words of reassurance as she sobbed softly.

She needs him more than she needs me, Davy believed, lowering his eyes.

The tears that Davy had fought off with a vengeance just hours before promised fresh troops for battle. Hastily, and as stealthily as he could, Davy retreated to his bedroom, quietly closed the door, and waved the white flag of surrender. When he arose from his bed thirty minutes later, his pillowcase was drenched, his wiry body exhausted, his mind drained of any thought but sleep. He turned the pillow over, pressed his head against its coolness, and succumbed to the promise of slumber.

"Davy, are you all right back there?"

Davy started from his painful reverie as if his hand had touched a hot stove. He looked up to see Mom inspecting him through the rear view mirror.

"Fine," he murmured.

"Need a bathroom break?"

"Nope."

"I do, I do!" Anna insisted.

6

"I saw a sign for a Texaco at the next exit," Mom chattered. "I could use a cup of coffee, so we'll stop there. Davy, Anna, I'll let you pick out one snack each while we're there."

"Yes!" shouted Anna.

"Whoopee," Davy glumly chimed in, circling his index finger in the air for emphasis. *Wow! I'm supposed to get excited about that? How lame! Just like this whole trip is lame. At least I don't have to put up with Jim right now.*

Jim had gone ahead to the farm several days ago, towing with him most of what they expected to need during the summer. He needed to make sure everything was in good repair and, more importantly, clean enough for Kate's standards. He had told Davy's mom that he wanted the family's first day there to be nothing but delightful .He was going to make sure of it.

"Here we are," Mom said unnecessarily as Davy and Anna could both see that the car was entering the Texaco parking lot.

"I want M&M's," Anna said. "The blue ones taste better than all the rest. I eat all the others and save those for last!"

"They do not taste better, stupid!" Davy retorted, pushing aside the fact that he had once thought so himself.

"Do, too!" Anna stuck out her tongue at her brother. Davy thought she looked like a lizard hoping to score a fly.

"Ok, you two, stop the fight right now!" Mom demanded as she removed her sunglasses and glared at the both of them.

"Sorry," Anna responded.

Davy said nothing. He earned the "you know better" look from her brown eyes, the image of his, and mouthed a silent "sorry" in her direction. This seemed to satisfy her for now as she threw him a darting smile.

"Let's stretch our legs, and, Anna, make sure you wash your hands after you use the bathroom. You, too, Davy."

"I don't need to!"

"Try!"

He didn't want to try. He didn't want a snack. He didn't want to stretch his legs. He could care less whether Mom got coffee or not. And, he did not want to be heading for a place unfamiliar to him. All he wanted was to be back at the apartment, playing video games with his friends on his X-Box and computer, and going to the pool. That, for him, was summer.

As he exited the car, he looked up to see a large man in overalls ambling toward the door of the gas station. His hair was misshapen beneath a faded Braves cap, and his face was creased from extensive exposure to the sun. He grinned and nodded politely as he opened the door for Mom. Until that moment, Davy had always assumed that the photographs mounted in his dentist's office were computer-generated in order to frighten children into the importance of brushing one's teeth. Another myth was now shattered as he had trouble closing his amazed mouth when staring at the obvious vacancy in this man's orifice where teeth should have been. He wondered what it would be like to run his tongue over his teeth and discover as many gaps as this man had. Mom maintained her grace and composure and thanked the man as if he was Brad Pitt, Orlando Bloom, or, he hated to think it or say it, Jim. Davy noted that the man headed for the restroom and decided that he would not obey Mom's order to "try." He could wait.

While Anna used the restroom and Mom fixed her coffee, Davy listlessly regaled the snack aisle for anything that might appeal to him. Mom had said they had only about 80 miles left until they reached their destination and that Jim would be planning supper for them. He glanced at the clock on the station wall; it read 3:20 p.m. What would hold him over? He couldn't decide between the salted peanuts and the beef jerky. He knew what Mom would say: get the peanuts! But, right now, he wasn't in the mood to listen to Mom at all, so he grabbed the beef jerky. Suddenly, a voice behind him made him jump out of his skin.

"Wouldn't eat, those, boy; bad for the digestion."

Davy whirled around to see the large man with the missing teeth not one foot away from him.

"Learn to hold the door open for your Ma, too."

The man picked up a pack of M&M's, walked to the register, paid, and, got back in his pick-up. He sped away trailing a cloud of dust.

Davy, his hand shaking, put the beef jerky back and reached for the peanuts. Seeing his Mom and sister approaching the register, he dashed to add his purchase to the pile.

"Good choice, Davy," said Mom as he laid his packet on the counter.

"Mine's better," Anna preened, opening her M&M's.

"You'll rot your teeth out," said Davy.

"Davy!" Mom chided.

Davy gave her his first smile of the entire road trip, turned, and walked to the car with a glimmer of satisfaction he hadn't felt for days.

CHAPTER 2
LONG, HOT, MISERABLE SUMMER

After a short nap, Davy woke with a start. Having gobbled the peanuts and washed them down with a bottled water (Mom didn't allow sodas), he was suddenly overcome with drowsiness. Worried about the trip the next day, he had hardly slept last night. He wasn't sure how long he'd been dozing, but it must have been a substantial block of time. The car was still zipping along the highway, but the scenery had changed. The gently sloping foothills of the Appalachian Mountains, wooded and ancient, had replaced the non-descript Piedmont with its endless trees and scattered farms, punctuated in too many places by billboards and Wal-Mart's. Still a bit dazed with sleep, Davy blinked, yawned, and struggled to focus on the panorama before him.

The mountains rose and rolled like waves above the shores of lush valleys where cattle grazed or crops grew. Farm houses, most modest and in need of fresh paint, were scattered here and there like shells on the beach. They whizzed by a large barn, decrepit, its tin roof rusty, its leaning wooden side still sporting a faded invitation to see Rock City. Davy craned his neck to glimpse the view through the windshield. In the distance, larger mountains loomed, their outlines muted by a bluish haze.

Mom must have noticed his movement in the rear view mirror.

"Hey, sleepyhead, what do you think of the mountains?"

Davy honestly wanted to say *awesome*, but he refrained, stubbornly determined to remind his family at every opportunity that he was not pleased with the summer arrangements. He met his mother's eyes, or what he thought were her eyes buried beneath sunglasses, and frowned.

"You've seen one, you've seen 'em all."

"Oh, Davy, must you be so negative about everything?" she asked, with a note of exasperation in her voice.

"Yeah, Davy," Anna echoed in an annoying sing-song. "When ARE you going stop being SO negative?"

"When YOU stop being such an IDIOT," Davy retorted. "So I guess that means forever!"

"MOM!" Anna wailed.

"All right, all right! Davy, stop the name calling! Anna, stop the whining! I can't concentrate on driving!"

Davy and Anna acquiesced to a temporary ceasefire, but not without Anna's parting shot—sticking her tongue out at her brother as was her irksome habit. Davy rolled his eyes at her. He hoped beyond hope that she would keep her distance from him this summer. She could be such an intolerable pest. Why couldn't he have had a younger brother instead? Why couldn't he have been an only child? Better yet, why couldn't he choose the family he wanted to live with?

His best friend, Evan, had the most fantastic parents in the world as far as Davy was concerned. During the summer break, they allowed him to stay up until two in the morning playing computer or video games to his heart's content and eating whatever he pleased. Whenever Davy went over to spend the night, he gorged on brownies or cookies or ice cream, foods that his mother strictly limited. He tried his best to keep his eyes open and his wits about him until the automatic timers put all electronic devices to bed. He was only able to do this once in all the many nights Evan and he hung out together. It was just too hard as his bedtime, even in the summer, was ten o'clock.

Needless to say, Evan liked hanging out with Davy during the day, especially when they could go swimming at the apartment's pool, but Evan always declined an invitation to sleep over. This puzzled Davy's mom who had offered several times to host Evan at their house in return for the many times Davy had spent the night with him. Always the response was a quick, but polite, "no, thank you" combined with Evan's winning smile. The latter, Davy was convinced, prevented his mom from prying further and, after a while, she stopped asking altogether. She did, however, ask Davy why he thought Evan was so reluctant to spend the night at the apartment. Davy had to think fast. He couldn't let her know the truth, that bedtime was ridiculously early and the snacks stunk, because she would know why Davy was so eager to stay at Evan's house. If she ever knew how much junk food Davy consumed when he was there, she would forbid him to ever darken Evan's door again.

"He sleeps with a teddy bear," Davy had told his mom.

"What?" She asked, incredulous.

"Remember that story about Ira and the teddy bear that you used to read to me?"

"Yes."

"Well, Evan's like Ira, and he's embarrassed to stay at someone else's house."

Davy knew by the look on his mother's face that she was skeptical about the explanation, but it was the best he could muster at that moment. He didn't like the fact that he had lied to his mother, and placed Evan's reputation in jeopardy at the same time.

"You won't tell Evan I shared that secret, will you, Mom? He'd clobber me and probably never speak to me again."

"I won't tell," his mother reassured him, but he could conclude from her pursed lips and knitted brow that she was having a most difficult time picturing Evan, Mr. Personality, snuggled up with a stuffed toy.

Now, as the car purred along the scenic highway, propelling him ever closer to the "summer of doom," Davy found himself wishing with all his might that this was only a bad dream from which he would awaken at any moment to find himself in his own room, in his own bed, where everything was comfortable and familiar.

If only "Pokemon" was real, Davy thought longingly, *I would become Celebi and fly back home.* He closed his eyes, indulging in the fantasy of instantly morphing into that childish, playful character, seeing the shock and disbelief on the faces of Anna and Mom as he darted through the car window and soared up, up, up into the vast blue sky until he was no more than a speck in their sight. Magical powers would guide him home to Atlanta where he would land at Evan's doorstep and be invited in to stay forever with parents who would love and understand him infinitely more than Mom and Jim ever could. Anna's petulant voice disrupted his pleasant reverie.

"When are we going to get there, Mom? I'm tired of sitting in the car!"

"I am, too, Anna. Just hang in there, sweetie, I don't think it's much farther."

She was driving down a less congested two-lane road that wound through a valley and followed the path of a large stream that rushed alongside. Davy could hear the sound of it even with the car windows rolled up. Around a bend, he glimpsed a flotilla of rafters paddling with the current, their beaming faces conveying their exhilaration and delight in their adventure. Surprisingly, Davy found himself thinking that this experience would be one he could relish. He had to admit that the log ride, his favorite at Six Flags, paled in comparison. Here, one was at the mercy of rapids and the aptitude of a guide while the other, though it got you wet, was predictable and finite. He wondered how much it would cost for the family to take one of these trips down the, uh, down the . . . Davy could no longer contain himself.

"Hey, Mom, what's the name of this river?"

"Nantahala, honey. In Cherokee, it means 'Land of the Noonday Sun.' We're in North Carolina now."

"Why the name, Nantahala?" In repeating the word, he thought that the syllables sounded like sweet musical notes.

"See the mountains rising on either side of us? We're traveling through the Nantahala Gorge. The Cherokee Indians noted that the only time full sunlight made its way to this place was at the noon hour."

Davy was impressed in spite of himself. How did Mom know all this? He gazed back at the river and noted, for the first time, how the sun's rays cavorted and danced on the waters' flowing surface, dazzling his eyes. He pressed closer to the car window, anxious not to miss a single sight.

They passed more rafters and some kayakers. Soon there were signs for campgrounds, inns, mountain retreats, and places to rent rafts. Davy paid special attention to the latter. The one which looked the most inviting was the Nantahala Outdoor Center. He wanted to stop to get a closer look at the place, and watch the rafters plummet down a singularly large rapid, but he knew it was useless to suggest it. His mother was worn and frazzled with the long drive and was definitely in her *I just want to get there* mode. Anna, however, never picked up on such nuances.

"Oh, Mom, look at all the people watching the rafters! Can we stop, please?"

"Not now, Anna."

"But I need to stretch my legs!"

"You'll have all summer to stretch your legs, so hush! I'm not stopping."

Mom tossed her cell phone in the back seat.

"Davy, see if I have a signal. If I have one, call Jim and tell him where we are."

Davy flipped open the Samsung and checked for bars. They had all but vanished from the screen.

"Nope, no signal here."

"Darn! Must be the mountains blocking it. Well, guess we'll just have to surprise him."

The road had left the river behind and was climbing out of the gorge. Davy missed the river already and determined then and there he would ask for a raft trip for his upcoming birthday. Mom and Jim were routinely tight with the purse strings, but not on special occasions like Christmas and birthdays. If, however, they did balk at the cost, Davy would remind them on no uncertain terms that this would be the one and only bright spot in this dreadful summer, and they owed him in a big way. *They didn't even let me bring the X-box, for crying out loud!* This thought catapulted Davy back to his former sour mood. Not even a sign promoting panning for gemstones could cheer him.

"There's the general store," Mom's excited voice startled him. "Here is where we turn off the main road. Hooray!"

Big whoop! Davy slumped down in his seat, more disgruntled than ever. They didn't even let me bring my PSP. What am I going to do for the whole summer? He stared up and out of the window. Tree after tree after tree slipped past; nothing but woods, vibrantly green with summer-fresh branches, met his gaze. The boughs swayed and the sun-showered leaves rippled, belying a substantial breeze. *A hot one, no doubt,* Davy thought morosely. Exiting the comfortably air-conditioned vehicle, in what appeared to be a few inevitable moments, did not appeal to him in the least. Heat was one thing he did not tolerate well. *That house better have air!*

Mom slowed the car and turned right. Tires crunched on gravel and the shocks met their match as the car bounced and jostled its way along the uneven surface. Davy's curiosity got the best of him at last; he raised himself up in the seat so as to see out the windows horizontally. On the left was the mountain side peppered with trees; to the right, an alarming drop-off with more trees that clung to the precarious side with ferocious tenacity. Alarmed, Davy's gaze darted to the rear view mirror where his mother's reflection revealed her lower lip caught in the vise of her upper bite. Her hands, cemented to the steering wheel, boasted the whitest knuckles he had ever seen. Mom rarely swore, but Davy conjectured that her mind was, at this moment, swirling with epitaphs that would make a rapper blush.

It was obvious that Jim had not told her about this precarious approach to Grandpa Will's house and it was not clear as to whether she had ever told him about her fear of mountain roads without guard rails. Either way, Mom was not having a pleasant drive. Davy knew better than to say a word that would break her concentration. Even the usually clueless Anna was subdued, perhaps frightened herself by the imagined result of a slip of a wheel or the failure of brakes. Before the situation reached a crisis, the road dipped, hugging the mountain to the left, and wooden cross-tie fencing appeared on the right, giving the impression, at least, of safer travel. As the road leveled and they could glean the first glimpse of the farm, Mom breathed an audible sigh of relief as the circulation returned to her paralyzed fingers.

"Thank you, God!" Mom exuded.

"Amen!" Anna added.

Davy said nothing. Instead, he strained to see the modest fields and farm house that was their destination. He guessed, too, that Mom had not been cussing about the dilemma, but praying for strength and resolve to overcome her fears. He had to admit that as far as Mom was concerned, this made much more sense. Maybe he had momentarily supplanted his mom with Evan's who rarely missed an opportunity to swear at any unfortunate event or person who dared to deter her will when on the road. Davy found it amusing that when Evan was caught uttering similar diatribes, his mother promptly corrected him and feigned astonishment as to where he could have ever picked up such foul language. Was it possible she didn't even know she was cursing when she was deeply engrossed in the latest rude encounter behind the wheel? That was a thought for another time.

Davy's attention was now riveted on the bumpy road ahead which, between thick forest, allowed glimpses of the house that would be his summer home, like it or not. The car eased around one more bend and the trees became less dense, offering a clear view of meadow, garden and house. He could see Jim on the front porch, waving an ecstatic greeting. A look in the rearview mirror confirmed Mom's beaming smile. *They may be happy, but, what about me?* Davy thought sullenly. *It's going to be one long, hot, miserable summer.*

Chapter 3
The Chosen One

Mom slowed the car and parked it next to Jim's truck.

"Everybody out!" she announced gleefully.

Anna didn't waste a second, bolting out the car door in record time. Davy moved more slowly. He was not anxious to encounter a blast of heat after the air-conditioned comfort of the car. To his surprise, the temperature was balmy and the brisk breeze that he had witnessed in the swaying tree limbs earlier gave a soothing welcome to his face. He stood for a few moments by the closed car door, the truck obscuring the view of the house which, he had previously deduced from the road, was old but well kept; its freshly painted, white siding glistened in the bright sunlight. He shaded his eyes with his hand and focused on the thick hardwood forest in front of him. Since he had lived in the city for all of his ten years, Davy had never seen so many trees growing together in one place. Their heights were as majestic close up as the mountains had been in the distance, and the deep shadows of the forest floor evoked in Davy a sense of mystery and magic. Out of the corner of his eye, he caught just the slightest shimmer of something moving in the tree branches. He blinked and stared harder, but whatever he saw, or thought he saw, had vanished.

"Where's Davy?" Jim's voice boomed, breaking Davy's train of thought. "There's somebody here who wants to meet him."

"Right here," he answered, emerging around the back of the truck. Jim had one arm around Mom and the other around Anna. Davy knew that they had just shared a group hug, and he was glad he'd missed it. Beside them, however, the dog which Davy had secretly longed to pat sat patiently, tongue lolling in a casual pant.

"There you are," Jim beamed. "Come meet Maggie!"

Upon hearing her name, Maggie struggled to her arthritic feet, plumed tail wagging. She was a golden retriever with more gray than gold around her smiling brown eyes and whiskered muzzle. Jim stroked her lovingly behind the ears and Anna, not familiar with dogs, gave a few tentative touches to her back.

"She's so silky and soft!"

Davy simply could not contain himself any longer. Momentarily laying all resentments aside, he strode determinedly toward Maggie and wrapped his arms around her neck. This was his idea of a family hug! Maggie, basking in the glow of all this attention, greeted Davy with a series of slobbery, wet kisses.

"Whoa, dog!" Davy was laughing in spite of himself. "You have the worst breath on earth!"

"Can't be as bad as yours," Anna sarcastically quipped, jealous that her brother was so at ease with an animal that she wanted to love, but was just too apprehensive to follow through.

"Well, at least she's had a bath," said Jim. "Talk about smell! Washing Maggie was one of the first things I did when I arrived; washed her bedding, too. No dog has the best of breath, but the older ones suffer the most."

"You did laundry?" Mom turned to Jim, astonished, because at home, the washer and dryer was her sole domain. Jim willingly helped with other chores, but when it came to running a washer, he claimed a blissful ignorance.

"Yes, I did," Jim admitted, blushing. "Guess it's not as technically challenging as I made it out to be, but," and here he grabbed Mom around the waist and gave her a quick but tender kiss on the lips, "it's on the bottom of my list of chores to do, and I am so grateful that you take this one on for all of us."

Mom smiled up at him like a smitten teenager. *Gross! I hate it when they get mushy,* thought Davy as he continued to stroke Maggie, scratching her chest as he did with Evan's dog, Sport. Maggie responded agreeably by arching her neck and raising one paw as if to offer a handshake. Davy took her warm paw in his hand.

"Well, Davy," said Mom, "it's evident that Maggie has taken to you whole-heartedly. Aren't you glad for that?"

Davy was not just glad, he was ecstatic. Still skeptical about all the other unknowns of the summer, however, he squelched a verbal response and simply nodded his "yes."

"Well, now that we have our introductions out of the way," Jim said, "why don't we tour the house?"

"Oh, Jim," said Mom, "I've been dying to see the inside ever since I caught sight of the outside. It's so perfect with the wrap around porch and tin roof. I can't wait to hear what rain sounds like when it falls on that!"

"Mighty loud and musical, if you like percussion instruments," Jim responded. He took Mom by the hand and up the three wooden steps to the porch. He held the front door open for everyone to enter, including Maggie, who walked stiffly by Davy's side. It took a moment for their eyes to adjust to the darker interior after being exposed to the afternoon glare. As the living room gradually emerged from the shadows, Davy's gaze focused immediately on the enormous stone fireplace with its wooden, hand-hewn mantle and sprawling hearth. It spanned the length of the far wall and even had stone seats on either side. On a bone-chilling night, one could sit intimately with the warmth of a cheerful blaze. The unique fireplace seemed to be Mom's first focal point as well.

"It's exactly how you described it to me," she said to Jim, "but it's grander than my imagination pictured. It makes me wish that the weather was freezing right now so we could all have an excuse to build a fire and roast marshmallows as if we were camping outdoors!"

"We can still sit on the stone chairs," said Anna as she dashed across the room, over a generous, if worn, rag rug, to plop herself down on one of the benches. "Wow, it's actually cold when you touch it! Everybody come try it out!"

No one needed to be asked twice. Within seconds, the entire family, including Maggie, converged on the fireplace seats. Davy ran his hand over the smooth slabs of slate and marveled at the giant flue guarding the chimney. Anna was right about the temperature. It made him grateful that he was wearing jeans, not shorts, as Anna was right now. Although there were no charred logs on the hearth, the faint odor of burnt wood lingered as if permanently absorbed by the fireplace walls.

From this vantage point, everyone had a perfect view of the living area they had so quickly traversed. There was one oversized leather lazy-boy in a far corner with a standing lamp, its shade silhouetted with a motif of leaves. Built-in bookshelves crammed with volumes of every description lined that one wall, giving way only to expansive, curtained windows which reached from floor to ceiling. As the curtains were slightly drawn back, Davy could see that the panes were rippled, not clear and straight like the windows at home. Once again, curiosity won Davy over. "Why are the windows all wavy?" he asked.

Jim replied, "The glass is hand-blown, Davy. In the 18th and 19th centuries, that was the only glass manufactured, not like in large factories today. Every piece is different and slightly flawed due to human error. Still, you can see out of the windows just fine." He added, "This house was constructed before the Civil War, kids; that's why we call it antebellum, meaning 'before the war'. It's old, to be sure, but it's been taken care of well over the years. It was built by my great-great-great grandpa. Pretty amazing, huh?"

"And look at the wide wooden planks on the floor," Mom said. "They're nothing like the flimsy wood floors in homes today."

Davy and Anna both studied the floor for a moment. The wood was worn but sturdy.

"It looks like it was made from whole tree trunks," Anna observed.

"You're right, honey," Mom said.

While Jim enlightened them on the history of floors, none of which interested Davy in the least, he continued to peruse the room. There was an overstuffed sofa whose muted brown color was enlivened by a hand-sewn quilt draped across its back. On the wall opposite the bookcases were an imposing roll-top desk and mahogany side tables adorned with dozens of framed family pictures. Hanging on the walls were more photographs, one of which portrayed a young man with a serious face who was clad in a Confederate uniform, his rifle cradled in his arms. Davy wondered who among Jim's many relatives this might be? Did he survive the war to return to this house?

He thought of the picture he had of his father, smartly dressed in his military uniform, a broad smile on his face, a persistent twinkle in his eye. Davy had tucked the picture in his suitcase, intending to place it next to the strange bed in a strange house as a comforting presence. He looked again at the soldier who fought so many years ago for a cause lost to the south almost before it was begun. He didn't look much older than a teenager with his beardless, baby face and soft, smooth skin. But, there was something behind the tight-lipped mouth, the stoic gaze, that conveyed a solemn knowledge of life and death far beyond what his innocent years should have been able to measure. Davy felt inexplicably drawn to this young man, not much older than he when called to war. He pondered for the first time since his father had died, if he determined to follow in his father's footsteps, would he be captured in a photo looking as exuberant and brave as his Dad? Or, would his face show instead the maelstrom of war reflected on the face of this ancestral soldier?

"C'mon, kids," Jim interrupted Davy's thoughts. "Let's see the rest of the house."

"Bathroom first," said Mom. "That was a long trip and I have got to go!"

"Me, too!" said Anna.

"Well," Jim grimaced slightly, "there's only one, so you'll have to wait your turn. It's right down this hallway and before you get to the kitchen."

The ladies lost no time in hurrying in the direction Jim indicated.

"What?" Davy couldn't believe his ears. "Only ONE bathroom? You've got to be kidding!"

"You're lucky to have that," said Jim with a chuckle. "When Grandpa was growing up here, all they had was an outhouse."

Davy stared at Jim incredulously. "You're making that up."

"Nope," Jim assured him. "It wasn't until Grandpa asked Grandma to marry him and she told him she would as long as there was a proper bathroom in the house. Needless to say, he wasted no time carrying out that home improvement."

"How did they wash up before they got the bathroom?" asked Davy. He still thought Jim was pulling his leg about the outhouse.

"They did have running water in the kitchen, so they'd wash their hair in the sink and take baths in a large tin tub that they had to fill up with water heated on the stove. In fact, the tub is still here, but now it's in the back yard, loaded with dirt and full of flowers."

Just then, Anna flounced into the room. *Mom must have let her go first,* thought Davy.

"There's no shower," she announced, sticking out her lower lip at Jim. "I haven't taken baths since I was five. Baths are for babies!"

"We can fix that," Jim smiled at her. "I bought a shower head attachment before coming up here, but just haven't gotten around to hooking it up. It won't be the same as the shower you're used to, but it'll work for the summer."

"I certainly hope so," Anna replied, crossing her arms and adopting the most adult air that an eight-year-old could muster.

For some reason that Davy was incapable of fathoming, Jim seemingly had unending patience with his brat of a sister. *Maybe it's because she actually likes him and he knows it. Why else would he laugh at her silly jokes and put up with her snippy attitude? She's such a pain!* Davy's rumination was interrupted by a friendly nudge from Maggie. He stroked her head and scratched her behind the ears. She whined, wagged her tail, and headed for the front door.

"Looks like someone else has to use the bathroom," Jim laughed.

Davy ran to the door to let Maggie out.

"She won't wander away, will she?" he asked.

"Not a chance. She's a regular homebody, that one. She'll only go out in the woods if you walk with her which we did just yesterday. As old as she is, though, she tires easily, so we didn't walk far."

Mom finally emerged from the bathroom, hair combed and lipstick freshly applied.

"Jim, it's so quaint!" she gushed. "I love the claw-foot tub and the old-fashioned fixtures. It could use a fresh coat of paint, though."

"And a shower," Anna added as if Jim had not been properly apprised of this fact just moments ago.

"What? You don't like the sky-blue color of the walls?" Jim asked, grinning because he knew Mom's aversion to anything but earth tones in her decorating.

Mom wrinkled her nose and shook her head.

"Maybe you'll like it better when you hear the tale behind it," Jim said and, after prefacing his story with the reason the bathroom was constructed in the first place, he continued. "Grandpa not only added the bathroom for Grandma, he told her that she could do all the decorating as well. When she chose the bright blue color for the walls, Grandpa's reaction was about as favorable as yours, Kate, until Grandma explained why. She told him that it was his handsome, sky-blue eyes that first attracted her to him. She wanted the room," he added, "because he loved her, to always remind her of him and his devotion to her."

"That's absolutely romantic," said Mom. "It still doesn't make me care for the color, but, in honor of your Grandpa keeping it the same, even after Grandma died, I wouldn't change it for the world. It can remind us of his beautiful eyes, too."

That was something which Davy preferred not to recall, mainly because the experience was one he still did not understand. At the wedding, the first and last time that he met Grandpa, he was unnerved by those eyes, so startlingly blue, still luminous and quick, though the creases around them were deep with age. He felt when Grandpa looked at him that his gaze, though not unkind, pierced right through to his very soul. It was as if he saw something there that Davy should have already discovered, yet had not been inclined himself to do so. Inwardly, Davy had squirmed and had tried with all resolve to meet those eyes as little as possible that evening, but their mesmerizing effect proved impossible to resist.

Davy recalled the reception. He pictured Grandpa sitting in a corner of the church hall, one gnarled hand resting on a hand-whittled cane, a bevy of children at his knee. His face was tanned and weathered. He had a sharp beak-like nose that made Davy think of a hawk. His remarkably blue eyes were dancing beneath his white, bushy eyebrows. He was telling stories, fantastic adventures of talking animals and the person they befriended, that person being Grandpa himself. The children, with whom Anna had sat, rapt and attentive, were enchanted by the wondrous tales. Davy had lingered on the outskirts of the group, not wanting to seem too interested, *after all, I'm 10, going on 11, and too old for fairy tales*, but hearing enough to be secretly intrigued.

Grandpa's voice was hoarse with age and he had to stop occasionally to clear his throat, but that did not detract from the drama and excitement of his vivid descriptions. If the disc jockey hadn't announced that the music was about to commence and ordered the bride and groom to take center stage in order to share their first dance as man and wife, Davy believed the children would have stayed there, transfixed, the entire evening. Grandpa shooed them away with a smile when the first strains of a love song began. He was showered with thank-yous, and Anna even gave him a peck on his withered cheek before racing away to watch Mom and Jim and wait her turn on the dance floor. As Davy turned to go, Grandpa called to him.

"Davy, come over here a minute."

Davy halted in mid-step. He could feel the harsh, prickly heat of blush rising in his neck, cheeks and scalp, the kind he got when caught sneaking a forbidden cookie. *Why would I feel this way? Have I done something wrong?* He approached Grandpa, struggling to keep from looking into those riveting blue eyes. Just as he got close enough, Grandpa's wiry arm struck like a rattlesnake, gripping Davy's wrist with an urgent firmness.

"Tell me something, boy," said Grandpa, searching Davy's face with that piercing stare. Davy's soft brown eyes were no match. "What did you think of the stories?"

"They're g-g-g-good, sir," stammered Davy, his voice barely audible.

"You think those are some tall tales, don't you now," Grandpa continued.

"Yes, sir," he answered.

"What if I told you they're not tall tales at all?"

Davy's face wore a quizzical look. He felt the grasp on his wrist tighten. An involuntary shudder seized his spine.

"Would you believe me if I told you they were true?"

Now Davy was actually trembling. Jim had talked a lot about Grandpa and his famous storytelling, but he never even hinted that the old man just might be crazy. He knew he needed to answer Grandpa, but if he said "yes," he'd be lying and if he said "no," he'd hurt his feelings. The dilemma was, thankfully, solved by Grandpa.

"You don't believe I'm telling you the truth, do you?" There was an unmistakable note of sadness in Grandpa's voice. The hand on Davy's wrist relaxed but did not let go.

"Davy, look me in the eyes."

It took all the courage he had remaining to obey Grandpa. When he did so, he was met with the unexpected; those crisp, clear blue eyes glistened like sky reflected in a lake. The face, just moments before so animated and vivacious, suddenly revealed all the cares and woes that ninety years could inflict. Davy's heart leaped to his throat, choking it with an emotion beyond tears. On an impulse that had no explainable rationality, he reached his free arm around Grandpa and laid his head on his bony shoulder. His wrist was instantly released and the old man's arms embraced his step-great-grandson, held him close, for the first and the last time, all in one irreplaceable moment. A sense of passing time ceased, the romantic ballad faded, replaced by two hearts beating simultaneously, endlessly, agelessly, thundering as waves breaking upon the shore without ceasing. Over the din, Davy heard Grandpa speak softly, words that both calmed and confused.

"Believe, Davy, believe, for you are the Chosen One. Believe. Believe."

The words reverberated from head to heart and back to head. *What does he mean? I believe! What does he mean? I feel so calm inside. I believe! What do I believe in? What does he mean?*

Suddenly, the music replaced the thunder within Davy's ears, and he was taken aback to find his face was streaked with tears, Grandpa's suit damp with them. Grandpa was smiling broadly, the wrinkles on his face a testament to the many times in his life that smile was practiced. Davy found himself smiling back, still not understanding what had happened and, somehow, not needing to right now.

"Look at that, boy," Grandpa chortled. "We've gone and missed your Mom and Jim's first dance! It's our turn now, so help me up. I need to find a pretty young lady to dance with!"

Davy laughed out loud at that prospect and Grandpa did, too, but Davy was sure that Anna would volunteer. He was right. Anna eagerly took Grandpa Will's hand in hers and escorted him to the dance floor As he watched those two dancing together, so seamlessly and gracefully, Grandpa's words echoed in his ears: "Believe, Davy, believe, for you are the Chosen One."

CHAPTER 4
GRANDPA WILL'S HOUSE

"Davy! Snap out of it!" Anna was tugging on his shirt. "Let's go see the rest of the house."

Davy's daydream melted eerily away and his immediate surroundings returned in sharp focus. He wondered if his recollection, placed out of his mind for weeks, was invoked by this house that Grandpa Will had lived in all of his life. *Could his spirit still be lingering here?* Davy shivered at the thought and decided to, uncharacteristically, stick close to his sister as they began their exploration. He was grateful for the daylight that streamed through the windows with the wavy panes.

Following the voices of Mom and Jim, the children trotted down the short hall. Davy, glancing at the infamous blue bathroom for only an instant, burst into a large room right after his sister. It was both kitchen and dining room. A long wooden table with benches for chairs dominated the scene.

"Wow!" Anna exclaimed. "I'll bet 12 people could sit at that table. I've never seen one that big!"

Jim laughed. "That's because in the old days, people had large families, especially if they lived on a farm. It took lots of hands and hard work to run a place like this."

Davy wrinkled his nose in distaste. Just the thought of working outside all day in the hot sun was repulsive to him. While Anna ran around peering into this cabinet and that drawer, just as Mom was doing, Davy let his eyes explore first. The countertops were wide and worn, and the porcelain sink looked extraordinarily large because it had no central divider as he had seen in most kitchen sinks. While it appeared scrubbed, a permanent rust stain betrayed its age. There was a huge pantry which Mom was currently rummaging through, stocked with crockery, dishes, pots, and pans along with generous amounts of canned and dry foods. By the kitchen door, there were hooks on which to hang hats and coats and a substantial wooden box with a hinged lid which Davy would later learn was for muddy boots and shoes. Windows, higher and smaller than those in the living room, obviously newer as their panes were clear, lined the longest wall, and another large table with numerous drawers sprawled beneath them.

A sideboard, seemingly crafted from the same wood as the table, stood along the back wall. Both stacked and displayed there were dozens of blue and white patterned plates of every size flanked by a generous helping of cups and saucers. Davy had missed Mom's outburst of utter delight when she spied the unmistakable Blue Willow design and realized that these were no reproductions; they were antiques and quite valuable. The stove and refrigerator, Davy noted with some dismay, looked just like the ones he had seen advertised in a 1960 *Life* magazine which Jim had saved. *Could they still actually be working?* He wondered silently and decided to see for himself. He strode across the kitchen floor toward the fridge, thinking that a glass of milk would be really good right now as he was both hungry and thirsty, and no one seemed interested in fixing supper. As he reached for the door handle, he heard Jim's voice. "Yes, believe it or not, the refrigerator runs like a top. Must have been a lucky fluke when Grandpa and Grandma bought it way back when I was a kid. I don't think any of the modern appliances would last more than 15 years."

Davy peered inside. How small it was compared to the one at home! What's more, the freezer was actually a small compartment occupying the upper part of it. A thick rime of ice coated its interior.

"Hey, where's the ice maker?" he asked.

"There isn't one," said Jim. "This fridge was manufactured way before those were invented."

"So, how do we make ice?"

"You use these." Jim produced an ice cube tray and began to fill it with water. "You fill these trays up, slap 'em in the freezer and, in a couple of hours, you have ice."

"Talk about the stone age," Davy grumbled and reached for the milk carton. "Hey, Mom, I need a glass."

"Look in the pantry, Davy." Mom was checking out the stove and oven, making sure the burners fired properly.

Davy entered the pantry which was even larger than he had been able to deduce from the other side of the room. It not only contained the shelves of food and utensils, but a washing machine as well, not as ancient as the fridge, he surmised, but none too modern either. Next to the washer, where a dryer would have traditionally been, was what looked to be a stand-alone cupboard. Its doors were decorated with tin circles perforated with miniscule holes.

"What's this thing?" he asked.

Mom's head appeared around the corner.

"That's called a pie-safe, Davy," she explained. "In the old days, people didn't have plastic wrap or Tupperware to seal up their leftovers, or refrigerators for that matter. They'd put their pies, cornbread and the like in the safe and the little holes in the tin would let air in but keep the flies out. Pretty nifty, huh?"

"I guess so," Davy admitted, "but where's the dryer?"

"Look out the window," Mom said.

Davy went to the pantry window and had his first view of the back yard.

"A clothesline? Mom, how are you going to survive without a dryer?"

"I'll manage just fine, thank you," she smiled and announced to Jim that she was ready to check out the other rooms in the house.

Davy stayed where he was for a few moments, taking in the scene that spread before him. To the left of the clothesline was a large, flourishing vegetable garden, the entirety of which he could not see from this vantage point. He recognized tomato plants, tied to their stakes, their leafy stems groaning with yet-green fruits. Mom had always grown tomatoes in large pots on the sunny deck of their apartment. "Nothing like home-grown tomatoes" she would always say; she couldn't tolerate the store-bought ones and refused to buy them, so the only time they had fresh tomatoes was in the summer months. Davy would have to explore the remainder of the garden to identify the other vegetables planted there and would, he hated to admit, probably have to ask Mom to tell him what they were as his knowledge of plants was woefully dismal.

Straight past the clothesline, about one-hundred yards from the house, stood what Davy decided must be the chicken coop, a modest shed with a small yard enclosed by a wire fence and partially shaded by the beginning rows of what Davy would later learn was the apple orchard. He could see no chickens pecking around in their yard and wondered if they were nesting inside. *Maybe they're laying eggs. I wonder if they taste different from the eggs we buy at the store just as Mom says tomatoes do?* Davy pondered. He supposed that he would find out at breakfast tomorrow. On Saturday mornings, Mom always fixed a huge meal complete with eggs, bacon, which Davy relished, and pancakes. He felt sure that, even though they were in a new home, this cherished routine would continue.

To the right in Davy's view sprawled a large meadow fenced by a seemingly endless stretch of trees that grew taller and taller as they ascended the hillsides surrounding the farm valley. The gravel road continued along at the meadows edge, but disappeared behind the trees. Davy wondered if, perhaps, someone else lived down that road. No matter, he would find out soon enough. After all, there was nothing else to do around here except explore or read books, the latter never intriguing him much past the books which were required in school. Davy knew that his indifference about reading disturbed his literature-loving mother, but Anna's propensity for keeping her nose in a book, he felt, more than made up for his literary shortcomings.

"Davy! You have to see the loft!"

Whenever Anna was particularly excited about something, her voice took on a high-pitched, tremulous edge that bordered on a shriek. Davy turned abruptly from the pantry window to see her dashing away from him through the kitchen, blonde pigtails flying behind her. He shrugged and sighed. He'd have to see the loft at some point, so better to get it out of the way now. Davy had to admit, although grudgingly, that his sister's enthusiasm had stirred up more than his usual state of curiosity. He heard Anna's voice again.

"See, Davy! You go up a ladder! It's so cool!"

Davy, guided by the sound of her voice, ducked into a doorway he had previously passed unnoticed and entered another large room, as full of light as the living room had been and just as comfortably furnished. Through an open door, he spied a spacious screened-in porch and the backs of Jim's and Mom's heads as they sat together on a swing suspended from the ceiling, admiring the view. He could hear their voices, low and lilting, but could not decipher what they were saying.

"Come on up, Davy! Hurry!"

In the far left corner of the room stood the ladder, wooden and stalwart, leading to a platform with railings over the edge of which Anna's glowing face peered down at him. Davy strode quickly over to the ladder and climbed without a second's hesitation. It was as solid as it looked and only emitted the slightest creak under his weight. Reaching the top, Davy stood for a moment, blinking in disbelief. His mind raced back to their visit to the Atlanta History Center last summer. They had gone on a tour of the Tullie Smith House, an 1840's farm that had been restored and was filled with authentic artifacts from that time period. The trip up the ladder had transported him back over 150 years: the rope beds with their hand-hewn frames and clean, but aged, quilts with trundles underneath; a wooden night stand with bowl and pitcher; candles set in a wrought-iron stand; an ancient footlocker; hand-crafted rag dolls, one propped on each bed pillow; daguerreotypes neatly arranged on a squat bureau, and hooks still hanging from the exposed rafters where vegetables and herbs would be hung and stored during the harsh winters.

Davy suddenly realized that Anna had been talking incessantly since he had entered the loft, yet he hadn't heard a word she had said, so transfixed was he by the scene before him. It was her sudden movement in picking up what looked to be a wooden briefcase that stirred him from his solitary thoughts.

"What do you think this could be?" she asked as she plopped the case down on the coverlet of one of the beds.

Davy walked over to her and examined the unfamiliar object. It was flat on the bottom but the top, hinged to the side, was slanted as if meant for a writing surface. Gingerly, not wanting to damage it, Davy lifted what he now saw to be a lid. Both children gasped as they beheld its contents. Neatly arrayed in what appeared to be a silk-lined interior were pens for dipping into an ink bottle, several of the latter still unopened, a supply of wax and a seal with an elegant inscription, and stiff, yellowed paper and envelopes. The temptation to touch each and every one of these objects proved too strong, but Davy and Anna did so delicately and with reverence. The box emitted a mingled odor of wax and age that, while not unpleasant, was certainly unprecedented in their memories. It was obvious to both of them that this was a type of portable desk, but neither could envision for what purpose.

"Let's ask Jim," Anna said brightly. *Let's not,* thought Davy, but said nothing because the urge to know was too overwhelming.

"Jim!" she called. "JIM! Can you come up here a minute?" In a moment, Jim's head appeared at the top of the ladder.

"That's the 1800's version of a laptop computer," he told them when they showed him the desk. "Officers used them during the Civil War because they were small, lightweight, and easy to set up anywhere. That belonged to Grandpa Will's great-grandfather, the one who built the original parts of this house. I take it that you two are pretty enchanted by this loft, am I right?"

Anna's shouted, "Awesome!" answered for both of them, but Davy had a burning question he just had to ask.

"Why did Grandpa Will keep all this stuff? Why wasn't it given to a museum?"

"Davy, everything you see here has been lovingly passed down to each subsequent generation, and there is a story behind each item. I think the only things in this room that are not original are the quilts, though they were hand-stitched sometime in the early 1900's, and the candles which I just put in this morning. Oh, and the bed sheets and mattresses. Don't think Miss Priss here would care to sleep on straw tick."

"You mean this is going to be my room for the summer?" Anna's eyes widened and her voice escalated into that squeaky pitch.

"If you want it, it's yours."

"Do I ever! I love it, love it, love it!" Anna threw her arms around Jim's neck in gratitude.

Jim laughed out loud, hugged Anna back with one arm and clutched the railing with the other.

"Don't go knocking me off this ladder, Miss Priss, or my summer will be spent in the hospital!" he teased.

Not a bad idea. Davy's dark and sinister thought surfaced, and his face reflected his anger; but for some reason, its bite failed to give him the sadistic pleasure that other wishes to be rid of Jim had in the past several weeks. Instead, he felt just the tiniest bit of a longing that he could get along with Jim the way his sister did. This sensation was too new, and it made him feel uneasy with himself. Then a thought struck him like a lightning bolt.

"Hey! Where am I going to sleep?" he demanded, his voice a startling shout. Although he hadn't explored it, he knew that the room to the left of the front entrance was where Mom and Jim would sleep, and he certainly hadn't noticed any additional bedrooms. The last thing Davy wanted to have to do was to share a room with Anna, but Jim hadn't mentioned anything about having to share. So, what could the arrangements possibly be?

Acknowledging Davy's disrespectful tone with only the slightest reflection of disappointment in his eyes, Jim covered quickly with a smile and said kindly, "Why don't you come and see?"

All three descended the ladder in haste and with a hearty sense of anticipation, Davy's laced with an inexplicable trepidation as well. Would he like his bed? Would there be a shelf for his belongings? Would his bedroom even be in the house? He had a fleeting, almost comical, image of camping out with the chickens, and almost smiled at the ridiculous thought. Jim might secretly want him banished there, he imagined, but he knew for certain that Mom would never agree to such utter nonsense, if for no other reason than he would smell like chickens and bring their droppings into the house like an ant invasion.

Jim led them to the screened in porch where Mom was still sitting in the swing, gazing dreamily at the garden, the meadow, the mountains.

"Oh, here you are," she said, her face infused with a joy that Davy had not seen since the trauma of the move began.

"Davy wants to see where he is going to camp this summer," said Jim.

Camp? Davy felt no little confusion at this point.

"Close your eyes, Davy," Mom ordered with mock seriousness.

Davy did so immediately, feeling unexpectedly the butterflies of a Christmas morning. Mom's soft hand took his as she guided him, obedient and blind, to what must be the far end of the screened porch. It seemed like an eternity before he heard Mom grant him permission to open his eyes, but, in the split second before, Anna's audible, inhaled breath betrayed that he was, indeed, about to view something that would not disappoint.

CHAPTER 5
MR. AND MRS. FAIRCHILD

Davy opened his eyes. There, before his astonished gaze, was an official, army issued cot made up with cool, soft, cotton sheets with a Mom-inspired foam pad beneath and his beloved pillow from his bed at home. An army surplus blanket was folded neatly at the foot of his crisply made bed. Attached to the outside wall of the house, just above his bed, hung a majestic American flag. On either side, she was flanked with framed pictures of his dad on duty, in uniform, casual, and with his mother. A tidy, compact bureau adjoined the head of his cot where clothes could be amply stored and treasured photos easily displayed. A day-pack hung on the wall with water bottle attachments and every compartment begging for a packed lunch or emergency snack.

Beside the cot, laundered and fresh-smelling, was Maggie's bed, in which the elderly dog now blissfully dozed, raising her head only when Davy, fighting back tears, touched her gently, affectionately, meaning to please her as much as distract himself from the emotions that overwhelmed him. Above the flag, polished and resplendent in the fading light, perched a brand new BB gun, the one that Jim had promised to teach him how to shoot the elusive cans of Grandpa's day. He wondered briefly:

Why not shoot animals instead of cans? Isn't that what they had to do in the old days?

The silence was more than Mom could bear, but she was unusually circumspect in stating her inquiry.

"Davy, is this all right with you? If not, we can change things to your liking."

Davy turned to look his mother squarely in the face. For a fleeting moment, apprehension troubled her visage. Then Davy, taking a deep breath and a spoonful of unexpected thankfulness, relieved her fears.

"It's awesome, Mom, really awesome!"

For the first time in a week, Davy accepted Mom's loving hug without pulling away. When she finally let go, he saw that tears were glistening in her eyes though her face was all smiles.

"Well," she said, "this was all Jim's idea, Davy. How about a thank you?"

The idyllic bubble of the moment burst. For these few blissful seconds, Davy had assumed that all of this was Mom's plan; now, after Jim had seen how pleased he was with his sleeping arrangements, he could do nothing less than say thank you to the jerk. *If Jim thinks that all this stuff will make me like him, he's got another 'think' coming,* thought Davy. Without raising his eyes to Jim's, he muttered an almost imperceptible "thanks."

"Oh, Davy!" Mom admonished. "Can't you do better than that?"

"Let it go, Kate," said Jim. "The boy said thank you and I say, 'you're welcome, Davy.'"

Jim sounded cheerful enough, but Davy detected a note of sadness in his voice. This made him wince inside and he suddenly felt the first, faint stabbings of guilt about his attitude toward this man who was trying his level best to be a dad to him. Although Jim had been married before, he and his first wife were unable to have children, this Davy knew from overheard conversations between Jim and Mom. While he was on a tour of duty in Iraq, he received the "Dear John" letter informing him that, when he returned to the states, his wife would not be there waiting for him. Even Davy, wrapped as he was in the insular world of childhood thoughts and perceptions, knew that this must have been a devastating experience for Jim as it would be for anyone. The loss of his own father had prepared the ground for empathy toward others, though Davy worked hard, too hard, to suppress those feelings. Their presence too often left him feeling weak and vulnerable; in being strong for Mom, something he felt she needed him to be, he had no time to entertain such foolishness.

Davy heard Jim's voice again addressing him and realized that they had all been chatting on while he was lost in this last reflection.

"Davy, are you ready for some supper?"

Until that moment, Davy hadn't realized that his stomach was actually growling. Yes, he was famished, the peanuts having been digested hours ago. He wondered what Jim had fixed for them. He was a pretty good cook, Davy had to admit, and he apparently found it a relaxing hobby as well. But before the family could head out to the kitchen, the sound of tires crunching on gravel could be heard, faintly at first, growing more distinctive and grating as a car neared the house.

"Who can that be?" asked Mom, a note of surprise in her voice.

"I'm pretty sure I know," Jim said with a grin. "C'mon, everyone, there are some wonderful folks I'd like you to meet."

Jim led the way back into the house and out the front door to the broad porch where Davy arrived just in time to see a man and a woman climbing out of a green Ford Ranger. They looked to be in their mid-to-late fifties, judging by the tinges of gray in their hair and the gathering of wrinkles, or what Mom liked to call "life lines," on their tanned and smiling faces.

Jim trotted to the yard, shaking the man's hand and hugging the woman in greeting.

"Kate, kids," he announced, "Meet Bob and Susie Fairchild, our closest neighbors and Grandpa's salvation."

"How you do go on!" Susie protested as the three walked to the house. "You know perfectly well that if it weren't for Mr. Will, we wouldn't have the beautiful place we do."

She reached for Mom's hand, already extended in welcome. Susie shook it with enthusiasm.

"It is such a pleasure to meet you at last! We were so disappointed that we missed your wedding, down with the flu, I'm sure Jim told you, and Mr. Will depending on us to drive him to the big event."

Bob interjected, "What a relief when our son, Ray, offered to go in our place. He had a great time with your grandpa and talked about the adventure for weeks afterwards."

He now grabbed Mom's hand and pumped with even more energy than had his wife. "Jim's told us so many great things about you and the kids, we couldn't wait to meet you all."

"And we certainly couldn't arrive empty-handed," Susie smiled and winked at Davy and Anna who stood quietly next to Mom. At that comment, Bob scurried to the rear of the pickup from which he produced a large, rather cumbersome, cardboard box. Jim offered his help, and the two escorted the box through the door, the living room, and into the kitchen where they parked it with a solid thump on the spacious dining table. As they passed him, Davy inhaled the unmistakable and mouth-watering fragrances of spicy chili and fresh-baked cornbread.

"You shouldn't have," Mom protested to Susie when she, too, realized what the Fairchild's box contained.

"Now, how could we not welcome you all properly to your new home?" Susie put her arm around Mom's shoulder as if they had been life-long friends. "Besides, we're going to share it with you, not to mention a celebratory glass of wine!"

When everyone had convened in the kitchen, Susie, who knew this room like the back of her hand, began to bark orders as if she were a career army sergeant.

"Anna, napkins are in that cupboard. Davy, get the silverware out of the drawer; mind you, we need knives, too, to butter the cornbread. Kate, the wine glasses are in the cabinet right behind you. Jim, grab the grated cheese and the butter from the fridge. Bob, get busy opening that wine and the Sprites for the kids."

At the word "Sprite," Davy and Anna stopped dead in their tracks, gazes riveted on their mother's face which did, indeed, display an uncontrolled expression of consternation. Susie caught it, too.

"Diet Sprite, Kate, diet. No sugar, no caffeine, no worries. Jim let me know that they're not allowed soda at home, but don't you think that once in a blue moon, it won't hurt them? After all, this is a party, a welcome home party!"

Mom knew the battle was already lost. She smiled at Susie and said, much to the visible relief of the children, that, yes, this once would be absolutely fine. Cheers ensued and, with Susie's lightning speed at dishing up chili and slicing the cornbread, the group was seated and ready to eat in two minutes, men on one side, woman on the other. Davy was not thrilled to be sitting across from Anna, but glad that Bob had plunked himself down next to him before Jim had the chance. He eyed his Sprite longingly, entranced by the rivulets of condensation it perspired, assuring him of its icy coldness and refreshment. If Mom only knew how many sodas he drank at Evan's!

Davy dared not touch either it or the tantalizing meal before him until the blessing was shared. To his relief, Jim reached out his hands promptly, the signal to join him and offer thanks to the Lord. He dreaded reaching across the table to hold Anna's, but tonight, for whatever imaginable reason, she neither pinched nor squeezed his fingers as she usually did, using her nails to leave a lasting impression in his flesh, not to mention a painful aftermath. She simply allowed him to take her hand that remained soft, limp and at peace, resting in his. Jim's voice began, clear and confident.

"Father, all that we are and all that we have come from your graciousness toward us, however undeserved. We pray now that you bless this meal to the strengthening of our bodies and spirits that we may continue to serve you and grow your kingdom. In the name of the Father, the Son, and the Holy Spirit, Amen."

"Amen" chorused the thankful voices in unison, followed by several minutes of quiet as they descended upon their respective repasts, a mutual silence punctuated only by the occasional "could you please pass the butter" or "how about a little more grated cheese this way." When appetites' edges began to abate, and conversation seemed to be the ensuing promise, as if on cue, Maggie entered the kitchen. She made a bee-line first for Susie who lavished her graying head with massaging strokes and, employed to the dog's seemingly delighted hearing, every expression of loving baby talk known to man.

"Hey, Maggie!" Bob's voice called gently. Maggie trotted around the table and placed her head on Bob's knee, eyes filled with adoration as they focused on his face.

"And, that's just one more thing you did for Grandpa and for us," Jim's voice sounded hesitant, choked. "You took care of Maggie after he died. You took her into your home and never missed a beat with all the arrangements necessary until I could get here and until we could come to stay."

Bob raised a dismissive hand while stroking Maggie's head with the other.

"The least we could do, Jim, you know that. Mr. Will was like family to us, too. He always will be."

Anna's voice piped, "Can Maggie eat some chili, too?"

For reasons that she didn't quite understand, all the adults laughed.

Bob responded, "Not unless you want her tummy to be miserable, Anna. She's quite up there in age and needs to stay on her special diet."

"Oh, yes, honey," Susie added. "Be sure not to give Maggie any table food, no matter how much she begs. It's just not good for her anymore."

"But, does her dog food taste as great as this?" Anna stated, punctuating her conviction by scooping the last of her remaining chili into her mouth.

"Can't testify to that because I've never tested it myself," Bob quipped.

Everyone laughed, including Anna, although Davy was sure she didn't know why this was funny.

"Thank you, Anna," Susie said kindly. "I'm so glad you enjoyed your first dinner here in your new home."

"You're an awesome cook, Mrs. Fairchild. Just as good as my Mom! I didn't think that was possible."

There she goes again, Davy thought, *somehow always ingratiating herself into the adoring circle of adults. She seems to know what to say when the words escape me.*

He took another long swig of his soda and realized with dismay that he had already consumed more than half of it. He had tried his best to drink it slowly, but the chili had been hot and spicy, and he had needed so much of it to soothe his mouth. Maggie's sudden nudge of his leg startled him, and he reached down to pet the silky head and ears.

"Well, Davy," Bob noted as he poured the adults another round of wine. "It's clear to me that Maggie will be in good hands with you here to take care of her. She's one special dog."

Davy could tell by the tone of Bob's voice that Susie and he would miss having Maggie stay with them. Momentary fear seized him; they didn't want to keep her for good, did they? It was obvious that the dog was truly fond of them both and would, most likely, be as happy with them, he loathed to admit, as she would be with him. No, he determined, not even if they asked. This summer was bound to be lonely enough, but without Maggie, it would be unbearable. Still, he could do the polite thing and tell them to feel free to visit her anytime.

As if Bob had read his thoughts, he grinned and said, "It's a good thing I'm over here working in the garden almost every day. Otherwise, I would miss the old gal."

Davy was puzzled by this comment, and it must have shown in his expression.

Susie said, "By the look on your face, Davy, I am guessing that you don't have the full story of how Mr. Fairchild and I came to be here on your grandpa's farm."

Without waiting for Davy to say "yes" or "no," she dived head-long into the story.

"You see, about ten years ago, Bob and I traveled up here looking for land to buy so that we could build a place to retire. After talking to an endless array of realtors, we were not an inch closer to our dream. You see, either the site was unsuitable or, if it was, the cost of the land was such that we wouldn't be left with enough money to build the home we wanted and still enjoy a comfortable retirement. After a particularly frustrating day of fruitless searching, we stopped for coffee and a bite to eat at the old general store near the highway. They used to have a small area for dining; such a shame it's no longer there. Best egg salad sandwich I ever had!" Bob shook his head emphatically in agree-ment, mouth occupied with his third slab of buttered cornbread.

Susie continued, "Anyway, we were sitting there discussing our dilemma and asking ourselves where we could possibly go from here. It was then, an elderly gentleman who had been at the table next to us came over and introduced himself as Will Hunter and asked if he could join us. We were a little surprised and curious, of course, but invited him to sit down. After introducing ourselves and telling him we were from Atlanta, Mr. Will (I never felt quite right calling him plain "Will," just didn't seem respectful, and he never objected) asked Bob what kind of work he did. When Bob told him he was the head horticulturalist at the city botanical gardens, those sparkling blue eyes literally danced."

"What's a horticulturalist?" Anna interrupted.

"An expert in growing plants," Jim answered her.

"Don't plants just grow on their own?" she asked.

Bob laughed, "Yes, they do, Anna, especially weeds, but if you want gardens like the ones we have here, you have to work at it and know what you're doing."

"Getting back to the story," said Susie, "Mr. Will and Bob talked gardening for the next ten minutes; my suspicion now was that your grandpa already knew the answers to the questions he asked, but needed to know if Bob was on the up and up. Those two just naturally hit it off and, listening to them, I felt as though we had known Mr. Will for years and were already the best of friends. That's not something, children, which happens very often, especially with adults. With age often comes suspicion of others, even when they seem well-intentioned. I forget now, but somehow it fell into the conversation that I worked as a registered nurse. I watched Mr. Will's eyes grow even brighter and more intense as he looked right at me. Not being accustomed to his gaze, I was just the least bit uncomfortable, if you know what I mean."

There were general nods and murmurs of agreement around the table. Davy was transported once again to that moment at the reception when those intensely-blue eyes had transfixed him.

He wondered if Mrs. Fairchild was glossing over the "bit uncomfortable" sensation. He, himself, had been completely disarmed.

"Mr. Will's gift, as I realized soon (and was to witness over these many years) was that he could read people, swiftly and unmistakably. If he didn't trust someone, you could bet your bottom dollar that the person meant trouble. Obviously, and to our wonderful good fortune, Bob and I passed the litmus test of trust. Mr. Will drained his coffee at that point, placed the cup deliberately on the table, and said, 'I think I just might be able to help you folks out, that is, if you can help me out, too.' Remember, Bob? Those were his exact words! Here we were, seemingly by chance in this humble diner, but we know better, don't we, Bob? My mother used to call them not 'coincidences', but 'Godincidences', when something happens so miraculously in your life, that it transforms the very direction your journey takes."

Here, Susie paused for a moment to take a sip of wine. She was intently aware that, at this juncture, she held everyone's rapt attention and could afford a short break.

"What happened next?" Anna asked impatiently, expressing the thoughts of her entire family.

"Well, my dear Anna," Susie resumed, smoothly, "Mr. Will invited us to see this farm. It didn't look as spruced up then as it does now because, even though he was spry up to the end, there were many things that were getting more difficult for him to do both inside and outside of the house. Inside, the house was as charming and, dare I say it, as haunting as it is today, but begged a head-to-toe scrubbing in every corner and a fresh coat of paint outside. The garden was full and flourishing, but weeds were threatening to choke some of the vegetables. After showing us the house and the grounds, all the while regaling us with engaging tales of family history, Mr. Will escorted us inside the kitchen where we sat down at this very table we're at now, and heard Mr. Will's solution to finding our retirement home. Bob, you finish the story. Tell them what Mr. Will said in his own voice. Bob has a knack for imitations. You should hear him do Presidents Reagan and Clinton!"

All eyes were glued on Bob. Davy thought he saw an almost imperceptible blush emerge through the tan on Bob's cheeks, but, as though previously rehearsed, Bob stood up slowly, almost ceremoniously, and planted his hands firmly on the table's edge. After clearing his throat with a cough and 'harumpf', he suggested that his audience might do better hearing Grandpa if they closed their eyes. Everyone obliged. As soon as Bob commenced speaking, Davy felt an unexpected thrill course down his spine.

"'Bob, Susie, I know we've jest met, but I know good folk when I see 'em. I'm gettin' up in years and I can't handle this place on my own anymore. My grandson, the only one decent left in the lot, is serving his country, something that makes me prouder than anything in this world, so I can't ask him to help. I determined a long time ago that I would stay in this house, the one I was born in, until the day I'm called home. I need a gardener and handyman; I need someone who can clean, cook, and know how to treat me if I become ill. I have this land, and you need land to build on. If you're willing to help me with what I need, you may build on this land and retire as you wish."

The ensuing silence was palpable. Bob's voice seemed to have ushered the presence of Grandpa into their midst as if he had been at table all along, celebrating life with the people he loved. When Davy, visibly shaken, dared to open his eyes, he saw the tears that welled in his own standing in those of everyone around him. Anna sniffed loudly and wiped her nose on her napkin. Davy, more discreetly, did the same. Mom made no pretense about her feelings, quietly sobbing while Susie placed a comforting arm around her. Jim, not trusting his own voice, clasped Bob's hand, thanking him physically as words failed. It was Anna who recovered first.

"Mr. Fairchild," she began. "Can you tell Grandpa's stories? He told wonderful stories, all about the animals: animals that talked and did all sorts of heroic things. Do you know them?"

Now it was Bob's turn to have tears in his eyes. "No, Anna. I know that Mr. Will had tremendous stories, but as far as I know, he never wrote them down. I only know about them because of him telling them to children at church picnics. He never shared them with adults."

They are all true, Davy. You must believe. You are the Chosen One. Grandpa's voice penetrated Davy's very being. He felt the presence. He endured again the ambivalence, the denial, and eventually, the emotional peace.

With a voice, seemingly detached from his body, Davy uttered, "They are here, somewhere, Anna. We will find them."

Mom and Jim stared at Davy with obvious shock.

"Davy, do you think Grandpa could have written them down and placed them somewhere for safekeeping?" Mom asked with a hint of doubt in her voice.

Before Davy could respond, Susie piped up, "Kate, if anyone knows this house, I do. I've cleared every cobweb, scoured every sink, aired out each bed, cleared out chests, bookcases, and cabinets. If Mr. Will left anything in writing, I would have found it by now."

"No doubt about that," Jim admitted. "You both have been a Godsend, both to Grandpa over these years and to us now. Bob, I'm not much of a gardener, but I'm looking forward to learning, and I know that I will be with the best. Kate loves to garden and hasn't had a chance living in an apartment as we do, so this will be an adventure for both of us and for the kids, as well. Susie, thank you for preparing this wonderful dinner that made us all feel so welcome and loved, and for making sure that not one part of this house wasn't cleaned to perfection. I can tell that Kate and you have hit it off, as I knew you would, so, Bob, pour one more round and let's raise a toast to a summer of love, bliss, and great memories shared among the Fairchilds, the Hunters, and the Murrays."

Davy lifted his Sprite bottle, finally a smile apparent on his face which he actually meant to have on it, tapping in unison Anna's and the adult's glasses.

To his chagrin, the bottle was empty.

CHAPTER 6
TWO WATCHFUL PAIRS OF EYES

Anna was recruited, not to her liking, in clearing the table and bringing the soiled dishes to the sink. "Where's the dishwasher?" she asked, surveying the kitchen now with a more studied eye.

"You're looking at them," Susie laughed, reaching under the sink's counter for a dish drainer and fresh drying towel. "Here, Anna, I'll wash, your mom will rinse, and you can dry and set in the drainer."

"But, I've never done this before," Anna protested.

"Then now is the time to learn," Susie insisted.

Kate smiled and added, "How do you feel learning how to do what I did as a child?"

Anna, accepting the towel somewhat ruefully, said, "Old!"

The women roared with shared laughter, but Anna, not in the least amused at the ominous looming of actual chores, which were too close to bringing her soiled clothes to a hamper at home, wondered for the first time if this retreat into the twentieth century held any merit.

"Why isn't Davy helping?" she asked petulantly.

Susie responded promptly, "Don't you worry, child. His work will be cut out for him this summer, I guarantee it! I wouldn't

51

be surprised if Bob and Jim have him pulling weeds this very moment."

"Can't we at least play some music while we're doing this?" Anna asked. "Where is the CD player?"

"I have a better idea," said Susie. "Let's sing."

"Sing what? What songs do you know?"

"More than you can count, Anna. I'll teach you; and your mom, if need be."

Davy, who had conveniently slipped around the corner after taking his dishes to the sink, decided he didn't want to hear the impending chorus and, with Maggie, made a beeline for his room on the porch. Plunking himself down on the cot, his head cradled by his beloved pillow, he took in once again the marvel that was his sanctuary for the summer. He still could not bring himself to fully admit that it was Jim's thoughtfulness behind the happiness and contentment he now felt. Davy had savored his meal completely and, appetite satiated, now let his mind wander.

He found himself thinking that Bob and Susie were fun people to be around. Even though he had hardly said a word at dinner, Davy felt that those two would be easy to talk to, that they would listen to him, not just hear him, as most adults did. They were old enough to be his grandparents. Since Mom's parents died in a car accident when she was only 25, and his dad's had retired to Hawaii, the distance made family visits costly and infrequent. At least with the Fairchilds living nearby, he wouldn't be restricted to the confining companionship of his own family. That in itself was a huge relief.

Davy turned on his side and gazed at the view of the outside world from his cot, with his left hand idly stroking Maggie's back. The porch was amply shaded by a tremendous and ancient oak, one of three gnarly giants that protected the house from unwanted summer heat. The leaves were rustling now in response to a gentle twilight breeze, and a few birds twittered sleepily, nestled somewhere in the tree boughs. From this vantage point, Davy could see how enormous the vegetable garden truly was. He caught a glimpse of Bob and Jim strolling together at the garden's far end. Bob was vigorously pointing out this plant and that; it was clear that they were deep in conversation, but they were too distant for Davy to catch anything they said. Beyond the garden was an expanse of meadow where tall grasses waltzed with wildflowers. Beyond the meadow were the trees, starting in the valley and marching like endless lines of posture-perfect soldiers up the mountainsides that encased the whole of the small valley. The sun had already set behind them, its lingering orange and golden light transforming the trees lining the ridge top into silhouettes. Davy was overwhelmed by the sight, and a small shiver of delight that had no name tingled down his spine. He had no awareness of time passing until Bob's voice breached the stillness. The two men were standing just outside the porch door, and, Davy thought to himself, seemingly not aware that he was there on the cot.

"Jim, I have to tell you," Bob was saying and Davy, rising imperceptibly up on his elbow in order to see them, noted that his forehead was furrowed with concern. "I've never in all my born days seen anyone as outraged, as furious, as that cousin of yours when that will was read; never heard such a stream of foul language come out of any mouth, either, for that matter. It concerns me, Jim, the threats he made to contest the will."

Jim's face was serious as he tried to reassure his friend. "Bob, I've thought long and hard about that, too, but I don't see how he can succeed or that it would be worth his time and money to try. Cousin Ronnie's always been hot-headed, even when we were kids, and I don't think he's ever forgiven me for pounding the tar out of him in front of all his friends in his neighborhood in Andrews. I was Davy's age when that happened and two years his junior. My mother and I were living with Grandpa and Grandma at the time, and Ronnie wouldn't quit teasing me about not having a father."

Jim's jaw tightened with this memory; his eyes seemed to be lost in the past.

"Mr. Will told us about what your mother went through," Bob said, placing a comforting hand on Jim's shoulder. "The amazingly wonderful thing to me is that your grandfather and grandmother loved her through the worst of times. They ignored the gossip and the judgmental attitude of family and the community, both. That took courage, conviction, and unmitigated love, love they always felt for the both of you."

Jim bowed his head briefly. Davy saw his fist clench and unclench in the blink of an eye. He sighed deeply and turned to Bob with a smile more forced than natural.

"Bob, I know you have told me on many occasions that Ronnie would bring the wife and kids up here to visit Grandpa and pass the time of day. I am aware he was physically in Grandpa's presence much more so than I was, being in the service and all. I have to admit that, when the will was read, if I had been Ronnie, I might have felt deeply disappointed as well, not to be left anything but a 'good riddance' letter."

"Jim, that letter was more than Ronnie deserved, if you ask me. Sure, he came to visit, brought the wife and kids, gave expensive gifts to Mr. Will on holidays, but it sure wasn't out of love for the old man."

"I know, I know," said Jim. "He just wanted this property so he could put up more of his cabins for tourists."

"Bingo!" said Bob.

"To give Ronnie credit, though," Jim continued, "I went on line to look at those vacation cabins he built over near Pigeon Forge; they're really attractive and inviting. Came close to booking one, actually, for our summer vacation before all this happened. His construction and design team must be some of the best around."

"No, doubt, they're talented," Bob admitted. "But photos can be deceiving. If you wanted privacy and solitude, you wouldn't have had it there, I can assure you. The cabins are built much closer together than they appear from the pictures. I guess some people like that, but not me."

"You know, Bob, I don't know why I never thought to ask you this before, but did Ronnie's outfit build your cabin?"

"Not on your life! Mr. Will said he saw enough of Ronnie as it was and recommended another area builder renowned for his quality craftsmanship. I suppose when Ronnie found out about it, he was none too pleased, but, if he and Mr. Will exchanged words over it, I never heard. My suspicion is that Ronnie gritted his teeth and swallowed his anger, still hoping to persuade your grandpa to leave the farm to him."

"And, I can't begin to tell you how awed I still feel when I look around and realize that Grandpa trusted me to take care of this incredible place, at least until the true owner can do so, what with your help, of course." Jim placed a hand on Bob's shoulder. "You did so much for him; I'll never be able to thank you enough."

"Just having you all here for the summer, close neighbors, good friends - that's all the thanks we need," Bob assured him.

At that moment, the women emerged from the kitchen, chatting with ease, as if they had known each other for years, and Anna immediately squealed as she saw lightning bugs cavorting in the yard. She darted and dashed, trying in vain to capture the elusive creatures. For a moment, Davy entertained the thought of joining her, but to do so would reveal his hiding place, and Jim and Bob would know that he had overheard their conversation. He eased his body back down on the cot and closed his eyes, feigning sleep should the men come up onto the porch and see him there lying there.

Before this evening, Davy had never even heard mention of a cousin Ronnie nor his dislike for Jim. He tried to envision Jim at his age, punching out Ronnie's lights, and putting him in his place. Davy loathed Gary, the bully in his own neighborhood, and wished he'd had the courage to stand up to him but, as Gary was a foot taller than he and at least thirty pounds heavier, Davy had favored avoidance over confrontation. He wondered if, when Jim whaled on Ronnie, they had been closer in size. Imagining so made him feel a little better about himself and that, maybe, he wasn't the coward he feared that he was. And, just what had Jim meant by the "true owner"? He had told everyone that Grandpa had left the farm to him, and why not? Jim was his only grandson. Rightfully, it should go to him. So who was this mystery person? On top of all that, what was the story of Jim having no father? Had his father died? Davy's had passed away, but that didn't mean he stopped being his father. All these thoughts crowded his mind and confused him. He longed to know all the answers, but thought now, somewhat ruefully, that he could not ask unless he wished to be revealed as an eavesdropper. He heaved a loud sigh. He would just have to be patient until he could figure out clever ways to obtain the information.

"Davy!" His mother was calling for him from somewhere inside the house. "Davy, where are you?"

"I'll check the loft," he heard Anna say.

Davy decided to let Mom find him so that she would believe that he had been napping all this time.

He heard her footsteps on the porch floor.

"Oh, there you are! You've been sleeping? Sorry I woke you up, darling."

Whew! She thinks I was asleep, so now I don't have to lie! he thought with relief.

Mom sat down on the edge of his cot and tousled his hair gently, just as she used to do when Davy was little. "I guess this has been too busy of a day for you. Do you think you have the energy to get up for a cup of hot chocolate before you settle down for the night?"

"I think so," Davy responded in the best sluggish voice he could manage.

"Good, honey! I'll see you in the kitchen."

When Mom departed, Davy got up lethargically, his mind jumbled, not from sleep, but from too much thinking. He loved hot chocolate, another one of Mom's seemingly endless items on the "should-not-have-too-much-of" list, so this was an unexpected treat, especially seeing as he had already polished off a Sprite at dinner.

When he got to the kitchen, Maggie in tow, Mom was at the stove warming the milk, and Jim was spooning cocoa into coffee mugs. Bob and Susie had left for home several minutes before with hearty good-byes and promises to see them all again tomorrow. Anna, already seated at the table, had retrieved one of the rag dolls from the loft and was cradling it like fine porcelain, whispering to its soft and faded face. She was saying something about "best friends" and "we'll have fun." Davy rolled his eyes and snorted. Anna glared at him.

"Hey, I thought those dolls were Civil War antiques," Davy said. "Why is Anna even touching one?"

"This doll isn't from that time period," Jim explained. "It's a rag doll that my grandmother made for my mother when she was small. It's been too long since she had a little girl to play with her." Jim beamed at Anna, and she smiled back gratefully.

"Does she have a name?" Anna asked him.

"I'm sure she did at one time, but I never knew what it was. You're free to name her yourself."

Anna studied the face of her doll closely. Davy knew how long it took her to choose a name for any doll or stuffed animal and, often as not, she would change them several times until she found one to her liking. This could take all summer.

"Here we are," said Mom cheerfully, plunking steaming, fragrant mugs on the table. "Sip carefully, kids, it's really hot!"

Davy leaned over his cup, sniffing the heavenly aroma of chocolate. Everyone was quiet, tired but happy, after this long and eventful day. It was Anna who broke the silence.

"Jim, what was your mother's name?" she asked.

Jim looked startled and surprised. He hesitated a moment, almost as if he had momentarily forgotten it or simply hadn't said it in so many years that the name caught in his throat.

"Mary," he answered at last. "Her name was Mary."

"Good," Anna said triumphantly. "Then I shall call the doll, Mary."

Davy thought he saw Jim's eyes glisten ever so minutely. Mom reached over and squeezed his hand. No one spoke for the next several minutes, but feigned an undue interest in their hot chocolates. Davy was the first to drain his cup.

"Take that to the sink, Davy, and soak it, please," Mom said with a sudden briskness. "Then run to the bathroom, brush your teeth, and get ready for bed. Anna, hurry up and finish that, honey, it's already past your bedtime!"

Feeling more tired than he wished to admit, Davy did as Mom asked. He had just rinsed the mug and placed it in the drainer when a raucous clanging of a manic bell made him jump in fright. Anna almost fell off the bench at the unaccustomed, alarming sound. Jim got up from the table, laughing uncontrollably, strode over to the sideboard, and picked up a black, club-like object with a curly-cue cord attached to it. Davy wondered what it was and why he had not noticed it when he had first explored the kitchen.

"Ha-ha-ha, hello?" Jim spoke jovially into the object. Davy could hear a muffled voice speaking to Jim. *A telephone? It had to be!* Davy and Anna walked slowly toward where Jim was standing and sidled up for a better look.

"Yes, yes," Jim was saying. "Will do. Yes, we all had a wonderful time. See you tomorrow. Good-night, now."

Jim replaced the club on its base, a cumbersome, black instrument that had a dial on it with numbers and letters visible beneath what appeared to be finger-sized holes.

"That was Susie, Kate," Jim announced. "Said she forgot all about her doctor's appointment tomorrow morning, but will drop by sometime in the afternoon to give you those recipes."

"Wonderful," said Mom who was now standing at the sink doing yet another round of dishes.

"Is that a phone?" Davy finally found his voice.

"Yes, Davy," Jim smiled. "One very old one when you look at today's technology. Still works, though, and, as I'm sure we've all noticed by now, Grandpa was not one to go in for, as he would have called them, "new-fangled" gadgets. Sorry it startled you both. We forgot to show this to you earlier today."

"How do you call someone?" Anna asked.

Davy thought he had already figured that out. "You put your finger in the holes of each number and press down, duh!"

"Uh, not quite," Jim corrected him. "If you want to call someone, you don't press down, you dial, like this."

Jim proceeded to demonstrate. The phone made odd clicking sounds as Jim pulled it in one direction and let it fall back in place.

"But that takes forever!" Davy exclaimed. "Mom, were these around when you were little?"

"Yes, Davy, but there were push button phones, too; some people just persisted in hanging on to the older models. If it wasn't broken, why replace it?"

Davy gazed again at the antiquated object whose ring was loud enough to wake the dead. "You know," he observed, "this gives a whole new meaning to the words 'dial-up.'"

"You're absolutely correct," said Jim, laughing again and, this time, joined by Mom.

"Ok, you two," she said, still chuckling, it's now almost past Davy's bedtime and neither of you have even made a start. Go, go, go!"

Davy and Anna raced off to the blue bathroom where they found their toothbrushes and paste neatly arrayed and fresh towels hung on hooks. They managed to accomplish this task with a minimal amount of elbowing and threats by Davy to spit toothpaste in Anna's hair. She countered by saying she would scream for Mom. Hands and faces scrubbed along with their teeth, Anna headed for the loft and Davy to the porch to don pajamas to wait for the nightly routine of prayers, hugs and kisses, and wishes for sweet dreams. Davy's pajamas, his preferred T-shirt and shorts, were laid out on the cot. Maggie had already settled in her bed for the night, and Jim had filled her water bowl. Davy realized suddenly that he had forgotten to ask when and how Maggie was to be fed, but figured he'd find out in the morning. She seemed more than content enough for now.

Davy dressed for bed, leaving his dirty clothes in a heap on the floor as there had been no instruction as to what else he should do with them. He crawled under the cool, sweet-smelling sheets and adjusted his pillow to suit him. Night had settled in and he found himself drawn to its myriad of sounds, so different from the daytime. Crickets chirped incessantly; frogs called from the stream nearby and, far away in the distance, he thought he heard the haunting hoot of an owl. Momentarily, Davy worried as to whether or not this symphony of nature would prevent him from sleep, used as he was to his quiet, air-conditioned room at home.

As he lay there, waiting for Mom to make her rounds, he decided he liked what he heard, finding the rhythmic flow and ebb of the creatures' voices unexpectedly soothing. Davy glimpsed through the boughs of the sprawling oak, the twinkling stars, vast in their numbers. They seemed to nod and wave at him as if each were the dearest of friends. Davy had only seen the heavens like this once before when Mom had taken them to the Fernbank Planetarium, not far from home. He remembered wondering if the stars were real as he had never seen so many of them before. Mom had explained that light pollution from the city hid the night sky and that only the brightest stars, like the ones in the Big Dipper, could be discerned. So entranced was he by the heavens' miraculous display, Davy didn't hear Jim walk onto the porch until his body blocked his view. Strictly out of habit, Davy turned away, now facing the wall, a silent and brooding treatment he was accustomed to giving Jim at home whenever his stepfather attempted to, as he interpreted it, invade his space.

Here, at this juncture, the feelings inexplicably drained from him. It was as if a huge and mighty hand was gently, but unyieldingly, beckoning his body to return to its original position. Davy discovered to his surprise that he was now meeting Jim's gaze. Momentarily, looking into those eyes, Davy wondered why Jim's eyes were a soft green, the same hue as his own father's, not the startlingly blue that Jim's grandfather's had been.

"Hi, Davy," Jim spoke, barely above a whisper. "I thought you might be able to use this out here at night."

In Jim's outstretched hand was a heavy-duty flashlight, its outside plastered in camouflage design. Jim flipped it on briefly to display the power it had, then quickly turned it off. He handed the flashlight to Davy who accepted it without hesitation.

"No street lights out here," Jim observed, turning to admire the indescribable array of stars in the sky. "No neon lights, no city-light pollution, only the light of stars and moon. That will be rising later tonight if you happen to wake up. With all the lights off in the house, I thought, if you woke up in the middle of the night, you might find this helpful."

A voice within Davy longed to say thank you, but his will, suddenly stubborn, held its ground.

"Where's Mom?" he asked, no longer able to look Jim in the face.

"She's unbraiding and brushing Anna's hair and telling her a bedtime story up in the loft. She'll be here as soon as she can."

There passed several moments of uncomfortable silence. Davy couldn't speak as his inward struggle seemed to tear him limb from limb. He wanted to ask Jim a million things; he needed to know the answers to the questions pounding in his head. He knew, now, beyond a shadow of a doubt, that Jim loved him. He wanted to trust Jim, so why, when he broached that seemingly unattainable desire, did detours and roadblocks in his mind hinder it from becoming reality? Why could he not simply accept the way things were and, at long last, be at peace?

"I'm here, I'm here," Davy heard Mom's weary voice announce. She approached quickly, pausing a moment to hug Jim and to let his kiss linger on her forehead.

"I'm whipped, too," said Jim. "See you in a minute?"

Mom smiled and nodded. Jim retreated, shoulders drooping, the weight of the world finding a convenient place to rest. Mom, a look of consternation on her face, sat down once again on the edge of Davy's cot.

"Have you said your prayers, Davy?"

"Not yet, Mom, but I will."

"Do you want me to say some with you?"

"No, I think I know how to do that on my own."

"I've no doubt you know how to do it on your own, honey, but will you?"

Davy nodded the affirmative; then he thought to ask, "Mom, will we go to church this summer?"

"We could visit the church the Fairchilds attend. At least we could sit with friends and feel comfortable right away. I think, since Susie has already invited us, it would be the right thing to do."

"Mom, I don't mind going with them, but, I have to admit, I don't find church much fun."

"Davy, not everything in this world is meant to be fun. Church is about community, Christ's family, gathering together to celebrate and to worship, to help each other understand the great gift we have been given in God's son. It's always a reason for fireworks, but that's not always communicated. It's almost never going to look like the latest video game; speaking of which . . ." Mom revealed the contents in the hand she had kept behind her back until now, "I thought this might help you relax tonight and feel more at home."

Davy stared in disbelief. There, in Mom's proffered hand, was his beloved PSP! She had insisted that he leave it back at the apartment, yet, she had brought it herself, and now gave him permission to use it against the unfamiliar background of crickets, frogs, and stars.

He grabbed it eagerly, placed it on his side bureau, and reached up, with both arms, to embrace his Mom with a smothering hug. Mom returned his affection and, with a loving smile, wished him sweet dreams.

"I trust that this won't keep you up too late, Davy," she warned before departing. "Tomorrow is going to be a busy day for us all once again."

As Davy's hand reached for the PSP, she intercepted it and gave him a loving touch. "Thank you so much, Mom!" he grinned back. "This is awesome!"

Mom responded, "'What father whose son asked for bread would give him a stone?' Blessings, Davy. Sleep tight!"

"Night," Davy said and eagerly switched on his coveted toy.

If Davy had not been so engrossed in his *PocoRoco* game, he may have seen two watchful pairs of eyes gazing down at him from the oak tree's lower branches. In the almost compete darkness, the flickering light from his screen illuminated his face, giving the illusion that it glowed from an inner source.

Davy thought he heard the faintest hooting of an owl close by, but paid little heed. The game enthralled him and he played with gusto. After about five minutes, he noticed that his fingers began slipping on the controls and the figures on the screen swam dizzily before his eyes whose lids he could scarcely force open. Davy tried to shake himself awake, blinking frantically; he had been exhausted before, but never had he felt such a stupor overcome him so quickly. The PSP slipped out of his hands and clattered to the floor. His limbs had become so heavy and inert; Davy could not make himself lean out of bed to retrieve it. His eyes closed and sleep overcame him.

As Davy slumbered, a melodious voice said softly, "There he is, my friend: Our Chosen One."

Chapter 7
The Forgotten Feather

Davy awoke the next morning to a myriad of bird songs and the savory aromas of coffee and bacon in the air. He lay on his cot, blinking his eyes, having momentarily forgotten that he was not home in his own room and in his own bed. The sky was filled with a pale, morning glow as the sun had yet to crest the mountain tops. Davy stretched and noticed with some surprise that every muscle in his body seemed both relaxed yet full of energy. He felt more rested than ever before and calmer inside than he had been in weeks. He tried in vain to locate the sensations of anger that had fueled his resentment toward Jim, toward Mom, toward the entire world. They had vanished. In their place was an indescribable peace.

An unbidden smile brightened Davy's face. That was the moment Mom happened to pop her head around the corner.

"Good, you're awake. My, don't we look happy this morning!"

Davy shrugged, but his smile didn't fade.

"Breakfast in five minutes, okay?"

Mom retreated to the kitchen. Davy threw back his covers and jumped out of bed. Maggie was not on her mat.

Probably in the kitchen, begging. I wonder if she's been fed this morning? Hastily, Davy got dressed and haphazardly made up his cot. It was then that he noticed his PSP sitting on top of his plastic storage drawers. Vaguely, as if it had occurred in a dream, he seemed to recall that it had fallen from his weary hands onto the floor. He hadn't even had the strength or ability to turn it off before it slipped away. Now, here it was, turned off, its screen shiny as if someone had carefully polished it. Davy scratched his head, wondering if Mom had found it this morning and placed it here. He'd have to ask.

"It's on the table!" Mom called.

Davy didn't need a further invitation. He dashed into the kitchen to find Jim and Anna already seated at the table and Maggie's head buried in her food bowl.

"I thought I was supposed to feed the dog," he said as he sat down.

"We tried to wait until you got out here, honey," Mom told him, "but with the smell of breakfast, she wouldn't stop whining. I just had to give in."

Mom refreshed her coffee before sitting down with the family. Jim said the blessing, and everyone dove in as if the feast of the previous evening was a distant memory. It was Mom's traditional Saturday morning spread, the family's weekly splurge. For some reason, Davy thought that everything tasted better than usual, even the eggs.

"Are these the eggs from Grandpa's chickens?" he asked, anxious to find out if his theory from the previous day was true.

"Actually, no," answered Mom. "I decided to use up the store-bought ones we brought first."

"I just wondered because everything this morning tastes different," Davy said. "I mean, it's always great, but today it tastes better than ever!"

Mom grinned and Jim said, "I think that might be due to your sleeping out in the fresh air; nothing like it to give a healthy boost to your appetite."

Davy didn't think that was it, but decided against saying anything. Somehow, the thought of an argument, even with Anna right now, was distasteful. He helped himself to another pancake, a strip of bacon, and a spoonful of scrambled eggs. If he had been looking up from his plate, Davy would have witnessed Mom and Jim exchange bewildered glances at the turn for the better his behavior seemingly took overnight.

"Keep your fingers crossed," Mom said to Jim.

"What about?" Anna asked, wiping Mary's mouth. She was pretending to feed the doll a bite of food for every one she herself ate.

"Never you mind, young lady," Mom told her.

"Kate," Jim announced as he stood up to take his cleaned plate to the sink and pour more coffee, "excellent as always!" He leaned over to kiss her head then sat back down, cradling his mug in both hands, fingers nervously tracing its handle. He coughed, cleared his throat, and took a deep breath before he spoke.

"And it's a good thing we've had this filling breakfast because I thought we'd all go exploring today. If you kids are going to enjoy the farm and the woods this summer, you need to know how to navigate."

"Yes!" Anna cheered. "We're going on an adventure!"

Davy did not respond immediately as his mouth was full. He noted, however, that both Jim and Mom were staring at him apprehensively, expecting, he felt certain, the Davy of yesterday to rear his ugly head in refusal. Davy looked from one to the other as he meticulously chewed the last morsel of his bacon and swallowed. *Oh! This is sweet! They are just waiting for me to say 'no.'* Then, uncharacteristically, he used his napkin to wipe his mouth and hands, got up, took his dishes to the sink, ran the water over them, and turned around to face the family. Anna's mouth hung open in disbelief; Mom and Jim echoed her amazement in their eyes. The suspense in the room was palpable. Even Maggie seemed to be holding her breath.

Playing the moment for all it was worth, Davy forced a frown, crossed his arms defiantly, and said, "I'll go, but only if I can take my soldier gear that Jim gave me."

There was such an audible sigh of relief among the family, that even Maggie lifted her head and gave a woof at the unfamiliar sound. Relieved laughter, shared by all, ensued, and Davy dashed over to Maggie to give her a reassuring hug and a welcome scratch behind the ears.

"Can Maggie come with us, or is it too much for her?" he asked.

"Oh," said Mom, "it's way too much for her. I'll stay here and make sure she's okay while you all go exploring."

"But, Mom," Davy protested, "it won't be the same without you."

"Yeah, Mom," Anna chimed in, "you have to get to know the place, too."

Jim took Mom's hand in his. "Kate, the dishes and the garden can wait. Maggie will be fine until we return. Come with us, please."

Mom met the gaze of each and every one of them with such joy that it made Davy wish that he had never done or said anything in his life to disappoint her. He knew that he had, many, many times, especially lately, but, with this inexplicable serenity within him, he wanted nothing more than to see his Mom happy.

Mom finally relented, "Okay, I'll come along, and gladly. I can't wait to see the property! However, I made breakfast, so I'm leaving it to the rest of you to pack the lunches. Here Davy," she laughed and added, "you're in charge of the napkins, now that you've demonstrated that you understand how they work."

"All right, Davy," Jim ordered with a salute. "Go get your gear. Anna! Help me get these sandwiches made. Davy, report back here promptly and be prepared for K.P. when you return to the kitchen!"

"Yes, sir," chimed both children in unison. And, in unison as well, were tears in the eyes of Mom and Jim, subsiding as quickly as they welled.

"I need to fetch my hat and sunscreen," Mom declared, giving Jim a quick kiss before she disappeared down the short hall and into the bedroom.

"And the binoculars," Jim called after her.

"What's K.P.?" Anna asked Jim.

"It's a military term for Kitchen Patrol, Miss Priss," he answered, giving her braid a playful tug.

Davy dashed to the porch and began collecting his pack and the water bottles. One of the bottles tumbled from his grip and rolled under the cot. He lay down on the floor and stretched his arm as far as it would reach. Grasping the lid, he pulled it out and, as he did, something else emerged with it. It was a feather, about the size of a quill pen, tawny with brown accents. Davy had no idea what kind of bird it came from or why it was laying forgotten under the cot. Deciding he would ask Mom later what sort of feather it was, he stuck it into his pocket and continued to gather up his things. That's when he remembered that he hadn't asked about the PSP.

"Mom!" he called as he re-entered the house.

"Yes?" Her voice sounded distant; she must still be in the bedroom.

Davy plunked the equipment on the kitchen table and trotted toward Mom and Jim's room. He realized suddenly that it was the one room in the house that he hadn't even looked at yesterday. Now, standing in the doorway, he was amazed at the size of it and decided that the furnishings, though old, were not as old as the ones in the loft. The four-poster bed stood so high off the ground that a step-stool was needed to climb onto it. In one corner stood a large wardrobe that functioned as both closet and chest of drawers. Mom was sitting in front of what Davy would later learn was called a vanity. It had a mirror at its back and two more on hinges, attached to each side that, when you swung them inward, afforded you the ability to see the sides and back of your head if you turned just right. Mom was sweeping her hair up into a pony-tail and taking full advantage of the mirrors' view.

"Hey, Mom," said Davy, "did you turn off my PSP this morning and put it on top of my plastic drawers?"

She didn't turn around as she could see him perfectly well in the reflection. "No, Davy, I didn't touch it. Maybe Jim did."

"Okay," he answered and headed back to the kitchen where Anna and Jim were wrapping up the sandwiches.

"Jim, did you pick up my PSP off the floor this morning?" Davy asked.

"No, I didn't," he said. "Grab those grapes out of the fridge, Davy, would you, please?"

Davy moved toward the refrigerator, scratching his head in bewilderment. Did he wake up in the middle of the night and move it himself? If so, he certainly didn't recall; in fact, he couldn't even remember having any dreams last night, a unique occurrence for him as he usually experienced vivid, colorful dreams and, less frequently, to his relief, lurid nightmares. And why, too, had sleep descended upon him so rapidly and definitively that he was inca-pable of resisting?

"Davy," said Jim, "you can't get the grapes if you don't open the refrigerator door."

He heard Anna giggle, "Yeah, Davy, take your fingers, grab the handle, and pull."

Yesterday, Anna's teasing would have precipitated a sarcastic comeback. Today, everything seemed different . . . felt different . . . was different. Davy opened the door without a word and handed the grapes to Jim who proceeded to rinse them off in the sink and then place them on paper towels to dry. At that moment, Mom entered, her gaze darting in every direction, assessing the family's progress in packing the picnic. She swooped down on the water bottles, lined them up in the sink, and retrieved a plastic ice tray from the cramped freezer. Davy watched her twist one to pop the ice cubes free. Two launched themselves out of the tray and onto the floor. Maggie wandered over to sniff them.

"Darn it!" Mom exclaimed. "It takes so long for cubes to freeze; I hate it when they are wasted."

She picked them up and tossed them into the sink. Then, she split up the remaining cubes as evenly as possible and put them into the four bottles, filled them with water and then refilled the plastic tray. For just a moment, Davy wished his bottle contained a Sprite instead. He could still taste the sweet, bubbly refreshment from last evening's meal.

"All right, that's done," Mom announced. "Now, do we have everything?"

The contents of the picnic lunch had been placed in Davy's day pack.

"Sandwiches?" she asked.

"Check." Jim answered.

"Grapes?"

"Check."

"Chips?"

"Check."

"Pickles?"

"Oops!" Jim hastily returned to the fridge to procure the forgotten item.

"Okay, kids," Mom said. "Let's all carry our own water bottles on our belts like this. See?"

"But, Mom," Anna protested. "I don't have a belt."

"Then, I'll carry it for you," Jim volunteered.

Davy hoisted his pack and was relieved to discover that it wasn't nearly as heavy as he thought it would be. It would have been embarrassing to have to ask Jim to carry it.

Besides, Jim had decided to bring his camera and gear along, and that was enough to manage. Mom was in charge of the binoculars as she hoped to see some new birds along the way. As for Anna, she insisted on bringing Mary.

"I won't get tired of carrying her, I promise," she said.

Davy shook his head, knowing that fifteen minutes into the hike, Anna would be pawning the doll off on Mom, but, once again, he kept his thoughts to himself.

"I wish Maggie wasn't too old to make the walk with us," he said, and crouched down to hug her neck. She placed a paw on his knee.

"I wish so, too, honey," Mom responded. "She'll be all right in the house. Anyway, the Fairchilds will be stopping by this afternoon and they'll look in on her if we're not back yet. Oh, no! They won't know where we are if we're not back in time!"

"Just leave a note," said Jim, giving his camera lens a last minute adjustment.

Mom rummaged in the buffet drawers for paper and pencil and hurriedly scrawled a note to Susie and Bob. "There," she said. "I'll tape it to the front door on our way out. Are we ready to go? Davy, you sure that pack isn't too heavy? No? Okay. Anna, do you really think it's a good idea to take Mary with us? Maybe she'd be happier keeping Maggie company?"

"No," Anna insisted with a pout, "she's happier with me."

"Then, we're off," Jim declared jovially. "Follow me!"

The four explorers trooped out of the house, each with his or her anticipation and hope for the day that lay ahead. As they walked down the drive toward the edge of the woods where the trail began, Davy found himself again reflecting on what he now called his "PSP Mystery." He wanted to believe he had put it away himself, but the lapse in his memory nagged at him as though he could fill it if only he tried hard enough. Walking made it impossible for him to shut his eyes and try to replay each moment, lying on his cot, before falling asleep. He sighed, resigned to postponing this mental exercise.

"Davy, are you all right?" Mom glanced back at him. "Why, you look like you're drowning in serious thought!"

"I was," he confessed, "but it can wait."

"Are you sure?" Mom's voice betrayed a note of concern.

"Positive," said Davy, reassuring her with a smile.

"Okay, honey, if you say so."

"Here's where the trail starts," Jim called as he was several strides ahead of everyone else. "Ready to enter the deep, dark woods?"

With these last words, he gave a roar like a bear. Anna squealed and latched onto Mom. Davy experienced a sudden chill along his spine, but its effect was not one of fear, but of excitement.

"Jim!" Mom admonished with feigned seriousness. "Don't scare us all to death!"

He laughed and grabbed Mom and Anna in a warm hug. Holding onto them with one arm, he reached toward Davy with the other. For a brief moment, Davy hesitated, but quickly relented. Enfolded now as he was in this embrace, he decided that group hugs weren't so bad after all.

"Wow! I've never seen your Sweet Sleep prayer work so fast!"

"That's because it had an added ingredient: Joy."

"What does he need that for?"

"His heart is not in the right place. Without adjusting that, it would be impossible to see and hear us, even if he does have the gift."

"Ah! That makes sense. But, what are we going to do about his toy? If it's not turned off, the batteries will die."

"Batteries?"

"I'll explain those later, Wise One. Right now, we need to set things right. Let's go."

Claws made only the slightest rasping against the trunk of the tree as a furry figure descended and scampered the short distance to the porch door. Silent wings followed and talons touched the ground. Had Davy been awake, he would have been startled and stunned by the two unlikely companions observing him through the screen door. A great horned owl and a gray squirrel, both twice the size of those normally found in nature, were assessing the situation.

"It's not locked," the squirrel noted. "If you can grab the handle in your beak and pull back, I'll slip in and take care of the rest. We'll be done in no time."

Wings flapped and beak fastened firmly on the metal handle. The owl's head jerked backward, and the door opened just enough to allow his accomplice to squeeze through. Without a wasted motion, the squirrel scurried across the floor to the PSP. After close inspection, the power button was located and the device was as dead to the world as was Davy at that moment.

"Give me one of your feathers!"

"Begging your pardon?"

Opening the beak caused the door to shut with a loud snap

"Yikes! Others might not be able to hear us; let's just hope they didn't hear that!"

The two were absolutely silent for several moments, listening intently. The owl assured his companion. "I hear the breathing of peaceful sleep. We're not found out."

"Whew! That's a relief. Now, I need that feather."

"Whatever for?"

"To polish up this PSP. There are fingerprints all over it."

"PSP?"

"Again, explanation to follow. Now, that feather?"

"OW! That hurt. Here, come get it."

"Open the door again so I can."

Slipping out again to grasp the feather in its mouth, the squirrel scampered back through the crack in the door only to have it slam on its long, fuzzy tail.

"My tail! It's caught! Open the door!"

His friend obeyed with lightning speed and the pinched tail was freed.

"So, so sorry!" the owl said. "Please, forgive me. This handle tastes horrible and I simply couldn't bear it any longer."

Inspecting its tail with tiny, clever paws to see if there was any damage and deciding it would only be sore for a while, the squirrel said, "No hard feelings, just a bruised tail. Sorry the handle's so disgusting. You only have to pull it one more time to let me out."

"That's one time too many, but, I suppose we have no other choice," the owl said with a deep sigh.

In a twinkling, the PSP was cleaned and polished by the feather. Next came the more difficult task of getting it off the floor and onto what the squirrel surmised was a nightstand. Luckily, there was a carrying strap attached. Grasping this firmly in his mouth, he strained and grunted with the weight but struggled valiantly until the task was accomplished.

"Whew!" he exclaimed, collapsing into a prone position, "that was NOT fun. I need to catch my breath."

"Don't take too long, my friend. The night is waning, and there are many journeys I must make in the time that remains."

Raising itself onto aching and weary paws, the squirrel jumped down from the nightstand and moved toward the door with uncharacteristic lassitude. He did not even bother to retrieve the feather.

"Hurry!" Wise One entreated.

"I can't hurry. Are you sure I didn't get a dose of the Sweet Sleep?" he added with a wide yawn.

"It was certainly not my intention. Perhaps you got too close to the boy."

The door was opened once again and the squirrel stumbled out, tail and all this time around, and lay sprawled on the grass. Within seconds, the eyes were shut fast and a faint snoring ensued.

"You are such a mess," the great horned declared, not without a note of affection in his voice. Looking skyward, he spoke wistfully, "I do hope I chose the right one of us to guide the child."

Then, curling his talons carefully around his slumbering friend so as not to inflict the slightest scratch, he spread wide and soundless wings, carried his limp cargo high into the limbs of the oak tree, and deposited the squirrel gently in its ample, somewhat messy nest.

"Sleep sweetly and awaken renewed in body, mind and spirit," said Wise One to both his friend and to Davy, though neither of them could hear.

With that blessing conveyed, the owl rose on majestic wings and vanished into the velvet night.

CHAPTER 8
THE ONE AFTER WILL

Had Davy's inclination been to look outside and up at the boughs of the towering oak tree when he awoke the morning of the picnic, he would have discovered the bright, beady eyes of a larger-than-life grey squirrel peering down at him. Smelling the brewing coffee and the sizzling bacon brought back to the creature treasured memories of many shared breakfasts and conversations he had enjoyed with Will. While he would eat the foods commonly consumed by wild squirrels, he much preferred, as did all his kind, the fare that humans prepared. Will's coffee had always been dark and strong, the bacon crisp and drained of fat, the eggs soft as melted butter on his tongue. The squirrel closed his eyes and squeezed back tears. Even though he was assured that Will was safe at home in Heaven, he couldn't help but miss his friend of so many years. Now, he had a new charge, a new mission, to befriend this young lad, Davy, and to introduce him to the world his great-grandfather, step or not, had known.

The squirrel observed Davy with a sharp eye for detail. He hoped that he, too, would fully understand what Will had seen in this child when they met at the wedding. His dear friend had returned from that event overflowing with the ebullience of a child on Christmas Eve.

"Grey!" Will joyfully greeted him when the squirrel paid his accustomed visit. "I have found him, the one to follow me! Come in, come in! Have a bite with me and let me tell you all about him."

Grey, as that was the name Will had given him, listened to Will's story with intensity and excitement. It seemed in the telling that his elderly friend's face betrayed the glow of boyhood, the lines of age fading as the light when the sun set behind the hills. The transformation in the old man was a wonder to behold. Grey found himself in those miraculous moments seeing his friend as the child he once was when first they met. Now, as Grey looked at Davy, he found in the line of nose, the shape of the lips, the thick, brown hair, the wiry build, the fair and lightly freckled face, an amazing resemblance to Will to whom the child was not even related. The most noticeable difference in the two was the eye color. Davy's were brown, flecked with green. Will's had been as blue and bright as a spring sky after a welcomed shower. Grey gathered by the smile on this child's face and the cheerful lilt of his voice, difficult to distinguish as it was now coming from the kitchen, that Wise One's blessings the night before had been successful. That was a relief of sorts, but Grey was still not sure of how or when he should reveal himself to Davy and, most disconcerting of all, how would the boy react to an oversized, talking squirrel?

"He's a doubter, that's for certain." Grey recalled Will's words. "But, it's been my experience that, once shown the truth, doubters become the staunchest and most stalwart of believers."

Grey had always admired Will's honesty and had often marveled at his friend's ability to size people up so quickly and accurately. Knowing that one aspect of Davy's personality, that of doubting, did not make the task before Grey any easier, but he prayed the end result would be most rewarding.

Suddenly aware of his empty stomach, Grey uncovered a stash of nuts in his nest and proceeded to nibble thoughtfully, wishing with every bite to be seated at the table in the house, partaking in a hearty meal. He was still munching and mulling over how he would handle his introduction to Davy when the boy popped back onto the porch and began gathering up his hiking gear. Grey inferred from this that the family was more than likely exploring the woods and possibly the lake today. Perfect! He could follow them in the tree tops, unseen and silent, observing Davy, and maybe the moment of revelation would conveniently present itself.

Grey jumped, startled by the clatter of a water bottle as it hit the floor and rolled underneath the cot. He watched Davy reaching to retrieve it and gasped when he saw Wise One's feather appear with the bottle. In his exhaustion the previous evening, Grey had left the feather on the floor and the night breeze must have whisked it under the bed. Davy seemed to be studying the feather closely, a puzzled look on his face. Did he even know from what kind of bird that feather had come? Grey did not think so, judging by Davy's perplexed expression. He watched as the boy shrugged his shoulders, thrust the feather into his pocket, and gathering up his gear once again, headed back into the house.

There was no time to lose. Grey swallowed a last morsel of nut, cleaned his whiskers with his paws and scampered down the tree trunk. He knew exactly the trail that Jim would lead them on; it was the walk Jim had most frequently made with his grandpa because it was so close to the house. Grey bounded across the lawn toward the woods where the trail began. Scooting up the first tree he encountered, Grey leaped from branch to branch, tree to tree, with ease until he arrived at one standing at the trail's head. Now he was in a perfect position to spy the family as they approached and be ready to follow them as they embarked on their day's adventure. All he had to do was sit patiently, watching and waiting.

His sensitive nose twitched rapidly as he sniffed the air for any odor amidst the myriad of familiar ones that might herald a reason for caution or concern. He detected none, as was almost always the case, but it was a long-ingrained habit which had, in some extremely precarious circumstances, served him well. Grey found himself recalling the Sunday afternoon, two weeks before Will passed away. They were sitting on the front porch together when he sniffed the faintest odor of cheap cologne mingled with sour sweat . . .

~≈~

"Will!" he cried out in alarm. "I thought you said Ronnie wasn't coming to visit this afternoon!"

"That's so," Will told him.

"Well, I hate to be the one to break the news, but I can smell him coming and the scent is getting stronger by the minute."

Within seconds, Grey heard the sound of tires on gravel, not louder than a whisper, and a sound that Will could not hear at all.

"Quick! You've got to hide unless you want to be stuck with that blustering fool all afternoon!"

"Hide where?"

"I know, the hen house! He'll never think to look there and, even if he does, you can just pretend to be collecting eggs. Hurry, Will, before they round the turn in the road."

The two just made it around the back of the house with Will making fairly good speed despite his limp and his cane, when the car made the turn that brought the house into full view. The house, thankfully, blocked the sight of two retreating figures bounding and hobbling toward the hen house. Ronnie would have only seen one of them.

When Will opened the door, the flustered chickens squawked, some flapping their wings in alarm, others trotting on their bony, featherless feet to escape to their yard. Will closed the door as softly as possible but, as there was no inside latch, he had to hold onto the handle to keep it shut, not the most comfortable of situations cramped as it was inside the little house which smelled of grain and chicken dung. Grey, instantly aware of Will's predicament, scanned the floor frantically for some sort of stick to lodge into the handle and brace against the door frame.

"Your cane, Will!" he exclaimed excitedly. "Shove it into the handle to hold the door! That way, if the bozo decides to look for you here, he won't be able to open it!"

"Brilliant!" Will whispered. Grey could be as loud as he chose as no one but Will could hear him, but the old man knew the same did not apply to him.

Within moments, they heard the slamming of multiple car doors followed by shouted greetings. "Hey, Grandpa Will, thought we'd surprise you. Grandpa Will? Hey, Grandpa, where you hiding?"

Grey had heard all this clearly.

"Ronnie's calling for you," he told Will. "I hear them. Uh-oh, now they're coming around back."

Ronnie's voice was joined in the call by his plump, unpleasant wife and their two unruly boys. Maggie, stirring from her bed on the porch at the ruckus, began barking vigorously. She disliked Ronnie almost as much as Will did, and she would always growl menacingly if the two boys came anywhere near her. She never forgot the time they thought it would be fun to kick her in the ribs.

"Well, if Grandpa don't hear that dog barking and come on out, then he's probably not here," Ronnie's wife, Betty Rae, shouted, trying to be heard above the din.

"Just to be sure he's not passed out or dead or something," Ronnie said, "I'd better check inside the house."

"Like you really care what happens to the old coot," Betty Rae retorted, in a low tone that only Grey could discern. Even though he knew that Will was fully aware of this family's insincere wooing of his affection, Grey was thankful that his friend did not hear this glaring proof.

Will groaned inwardly, deeply regretting having left the doors unlocked. The thought of Ronnie roaming the house unsupervised, poking his nose where it did not and would never belong, disgusted him. Grey patted his hand reassuringly.

"Don't worry, Will. Maggie will chase him out soon enough."

"But will it be in time?" The old man said, his face creased with worry.

At that moment came a loud thump against the side of the hen house followed immediately by another. The chickens, both in the house and in the yard, screeched and cackled with fear and flurries of wings flapped everywhere. Will and Grey instinctively ducked and covered their heads. Outside, the two boys howled with mischievous glee.

"Didja see them chickens jump?" one exclaimed.

"Yeah! Let's do it again!"

"Buddy! Sammy! Y'all get away from that filthy hen house right this minute! What a waste of Grandpa's tomatoes! We could have taken 'em home and had us some fried green tomatoes. Get on back to the car, now!" Betty Rae sounded furious, but more about the wasted food than anything else. She certainly did not make the boys clean up the mess they created.

Maggie's intensified barks let Will and Grey know that the three were returning in the direction of the house, but knew that they would give the dog a wide berth. Several long minutes later came the sound once again of car doors slamming, followed by the roar of an engine being gunned. Ronnie's tires screamed on the gravel drive, and Grey was certain that he heard a rebel yell as the vehicle sped recklessly down the road.

Heaving sighs of relief, the two emerged from the stuffy hen house, gratefully breathing the fresh air. Will eyed the side of the house where the remains of two green tomatoes dripped, their broken and wasted bodies lying pitifully on the grass, denied the chance forever to ripen. He didn't speak a word, but Grey knew that an intense anger surged through Will's body. The old man strode determinedly toward the house, through the screen door, stopping only to calm Maggie with a comforting pat, and began to inspect the house as if he were seeing it for the first time. Grey followed his friend in silent consternation. What had Will so upset, so worried, that Ronnie could have found, tampered with, or taken? All the legal documents were locked away in the Fairchild's safe, so that was of no consequence. An antique, perhaps? A beloved photograph? Why would Ronnie even want to take anything? If he did and Will found out, it would be the final nail in the coffin of any hope Ronnie had of being left even a scrap of the place after Will died. Grey figured that Ronnie was too smart for that.

After twenty minutes of close inspection, Will sat down at the kitchen table and closed his eyes. Grey half expected him to start snoring any minute. Presently, he opened them and said, "Everything looks to be in order. Grey, I don't know what I was so worried about, but something was urging me to go behind that varmint just to be sure. He's a snake in the grass, that one; never up to any good. All that searching around has worn me out. How about making us some coffee, Grey?"

Will smiled, then, for the first time in over an hour. Relief washed over Grey in a great wave at this sight. He never wanted to see his dear friend sad or troubled. He gave his best attempt at a squirrel grin in return and hopped up on the kitchen counter where the coffee maker sat.

≈

The muffled boom of a large door shutting and the ring of distant laughter shook Grey from his memories. He was immediately attentive, straining to hear if his hunch about the direction Davy's family would take was correct. Yes! The voices were growing louder! His whole body quivered with excitement and his tail twitched wildly up and down as he awaited their arrival at the trail. Thinking as he had about Will made him miss his old friend more than ever. The squirrel knew the joy that finding Davy had brought to the old man. It was all up to Grey, now, to insure that Will's legacy lived on in the boy. Unexpectedly, and quite unwelcome, doubts crept into the squirrel's head. *What if Davy and I don't get along? What am I to do then? Or, what if he thinks I'm not real and that he's lost his mind? What if he can't see me because he chooses not to believe? What if . . . ?*

But there was no more time for speculation. The family of four had stopped at the trail's beginning. Grey heard Jim growl like a bear, thinking that the imitation was actually fairly good for a human. He heard Anna's subsequent scream, then, the joyful laughter, and saw the family hug. Watching intently to see how Davy would respond, Grey chirruped with delight when the invitation of Jim's outstretched arm was accepted. He saw it as a portentous sign; Wise One's blessing had been strong and, in that knowledge, Grey shed all dubious thoughts and focused his sole attention on this child, whom he suddenly realized, had already stolen his heart.

Chapter 9

Awake, Aware and Waiting

"How's that for a bear hug?" Jim asked, his eyes twinkling, after the family had untangled itself.

Davy and Anna groaned at the bad pun, but smiles remained on their faces.

"Oh, Jim," Mom chuckled. "That's two-thirds of a pun, P. U."

Everyone laughed except Anna.

"I don't get it. Why is that so funny?"

"Think of the word "pun," Anna," Davy explained. "How many letters does it have?"

"Three," she answered.

"So, two-thirds of the word would be the first two letters. What are they?"

"P. U." said Anna. "Oh, I get it! P. U. It stinks!"

Laughter was once again shared all around.

"Well," said Jim, "I think it's time to get going. The valley trail is fairly broad and clear in most places, but there are a few rough spots. Why don't I go first, the ladies next, and, Davy, I need you to be the rear guard. We don't want an unexpected ambush."

Davy saw that his Mom was about to say something, but thought better of it. She realized that Jim was simply treating

Davy as if he were a grown soldier on a dangerous mission. Anna, however, glanced warily over her shoulders.

"And none will get through, Sir!" Davy straightened himself like a ramrod and saluted.

Jim returned the salute just as formally and declared, "Troops, let's move out!"

The journey began. Several strides ahead of him, Davy could hear Anna explaining the P.U. joke to Mary and then reassuring her that there would be no ambush because Davy was there to protect them. He had never thought before that anything his sister could have uttered would ever make him feel that she actually liked him or, at the least, held some shred of respect if for no other reason than because he was the oldest. Now, hearing her talk so comfortingly to her doll, a practice that just yesterday he would have belittled, moved Davy to a place within himself which he had not experienced before or since the time Grandpa had held him and whispered, "Believe, Davy!"

Momentarily overwhelmed and genuinely baffled by the return of that mysterious and moving sensation, Davy longed to cry, to laugh, to dance, to sing, all at once and all together. The impossible seemed possible, plausible, and, dare he think it, practical. *What had happened to him? What was happening to him? Had Anna really never offered him a praise or word of encouragement? Or, had it been his stubborn disdain for her silly, baby-girl ways that had prevented him from hearing anything she had to say?*

Caught up in this unexpected snare of bewildering emotions, Davy's pace slowed as if the weight of them had been added to his pack. It was the realization that Anna's voice was receding that shook him free. Looking at the trail ahead, he noticed it curved sharply; his family had vanished from sight. For a fleeting moment, he sensed a wave of panic germinating in the pit of his stomach but, just as unexpectedly as it had loomed, it subsided as the other, barely familiar emotions which had curbed his stride subdued its power. Feeling, instead, a courage worthy of defeating even his despised enemy, Gary, Davy decided to turn and scan the woods behind him to make sure there were no dangers before he trotted on to join his family.

Imagining he was in the same battalion commanded by his father in Iraq, Davy pulled himself up to his full stature and scanned the woods behind him; determined to spy any untoward activity or hint of trouble. Except for the distant and pleasant songs of birds high in the tree tops, nothing seemed unusual or out of the ordinary. Just as Davy was satisfied with his assessment and was turning around, he glimpsed movement out of the corner of his eye. He whirled back around, straining to discern what he thought he had seen. There! There it was again!

A rustle of branches high in a tree several yards away betrayed the partially hidden shape of what he thought must be a squirrel. Davy had certainly seen many squirrels in his young years as they are as at home in the suburbs as they are in the forests, but this one seemed much larger than any he had ever encountered. He rubbed his eyes, thinking that this simple action might erase any mistakes they could make, and stared again. Gone! His eyes darted in every direction, but he could not locate the creature. Where could it be? Had he truly seen something? Was this imagined squirrel the "something" that he thought he glimpsed yesterday?

Maybe it was just my imagination. This day is strange anyway, and I need to go catch up before they start to worry.

With that, Davy turned and raced determinedly up the trail, his backpack pounding against his spine, his water bottle flogging his hip. He didn't slow or look behind him until the backs of Mom and Anna were within his reach. Hearing his heavy breathing from his run, they stopped walking. Jim was about twenty paces ahead.

"Jim! Hold up a second!" Mom called.

Jim halted and looked back at them.

"Everything okay back there?" he asked.

"Think so," Mom answered, then addressed Davy, "Honey, you're all flushed! Have you been running? Weren't you staying right behind us? Here, take a sip of your water."

Davy caught his breath and savored a long, cool drink.

"I'm fine, Mom," he told her, taking another swig and replacing the cover tightly, "just got too involved in patrolling."

"Well, I'm glad that you're doing your job, but can you try to keep up, darling? Otherwise, we'll just worry about you."

"Yes, Mom, I promise."

And he meant it. As much as he, in the past, resented what he perceived as his mother's over-protective inclinations, there surfaced within him a fresh understanding. She spoke and acted out of love, nothing less and nothing more. Davy no longer felt that her presence was intrusive. He did intend to keep a look out for the elusive creature he thought he glimpsed, but vowed to make it a priority not to lose sight of his family in the meantime.

Grey was fairly certain that Davy had spotted him; whether or not the boy had identified him as some type of squirrel was questionable. Not yet ready to reveal himself, Grey shrank into the leafy shade and held himself perfectly still, not an easy feat for a squirrel. His tryst with Davy must happen at precisely the right time. Grey waited until the boy had disappeared down the trail before he dared to exhale. Then, he continued his pursuit more quietly and at a greater distance from the family than before, vowing to himself to be more cautious. The disadvantage to this was Grey could not properly hear their conversations; only occasional snippets reached his ears.

"Will you look at . . ."

". . . great picture."

"Let's stop. I need . . ."

"May I have . . ."

The word "stop" encouraged him. If he could catch up with them now, making sure to keep himself hidden, perhaps he could find out how far they planned to hike today and where they might be planning to picnic. Grey doubted that Anna would last the entire trail they were now traversing where it climbed quite steeply in places, but maybe she was stronger than she appeared to be. His hunch was that Jim would take them to the side trail that led to the lake. Near where the mountain stream met the lake's edge, there was an old picnic table, a perfect location for lunch that also provided a stunning view of the lake with its placid surface mirroring the mountains that surrounded it.

Several more leaps through the tree branches brought the family into full view and hearing once again. Grey froze to watch and listen unseen. Anna was seated on the ground, removing one tennis shoe and shaking it to dislodge an aggravating pebble. Kate had her binoculars glued to her face, scanning the woods intently for the pileated woodpecker she had distinctly heard, but had yet to locate. Jim was adjusting a lens on his camera as he hovered over an unexpected colony of foxgloves. Davy was . . . where was Davy? Grey wanted desperately to dash through the trees in a mad search for his soon-to-be friend, but he dared not move a muscle. Much to his relief, his keen eyes glimpsed the boy farther up the trail, moving slowly and deliberately, his eyes scanning the tree tops.

Then, he DID see me earlier! He believes I'm real! He's searching for me right now. I just KNOW it!

A thrill shuddered through his body from head to tail. He wanted to dance and sing and race up and down the tree trunks in celebration, but that would have to wait. Grey squeezed his front paws together and closed his eyes tightly.

"Thank you!" he said in a whisper barely audible. "Thank you!"

While his family took their break, Davy offered to scout the trail ahead.

"Don't go too far," his Mom admonished.

"He can't get lost, Kate," Jim assured her. "Just don't go off the trail, Davy."

"I won't," he said, and sauntered away as casually as he could.

Keeping up with the others and watching his footing had taken most of his concentration for the last half hour. Although he had looked up now and again when the opportunity permitted, he hadn't spied the squirrel, as he had now convinced himself that's what the creature was. Yet, he had a pervasive sense that they were or, more precisely, he was being followed. Davy imagined the black, glinting eyes staring at him, guarded from view by thick leaves and forest shadows. The thought aroused conflicting emotions within him. He was anxious, nervous, confused, yet excited. Butterflies seized his stomach and his heart pounded in his chest, its pulse racing in his ears. Fragments of Grandpa Will's stories whirled in his head: Fishing with the raccoons; riding bareback on a buck; an owl leading him at night to the rescue of child who strayed from the path and got lost in the woods, the squirrel who helped him harvest pecans and who liked to drink coffee. His tales had held the younger children spellbound, but Davy, never even assuming that they might be true, had listened with only a passive interest. How he wished he had paid closer attention at the time! Why had he not believed in the first place? His doubts before, so ominous and overwhelming, were now reduced to a wispy cobweb clinging hopelessly in his head as hurricane-force thoughts swept them forever away.

Could it be that he, Davy, was destined to have adventures and friendships with these creatures just as Grandpa had? Did he have the gift to see and hear things that other people could not? Feeling that his entire being had grown too large for his stature, Davy restrained with all his might the urge to whoop for joy and frolic wildly, just as, unbeknownst to him, Grey was presently doing. Instead, he strained his eyes to focus on the slightest shape moving in the branches above that would betray the presence of what he now knew was no apparition.

Shading his eyes from the rays of sunlight that filtered through the lofty canopy, Davy gazed intently, turning in every direction, dwelling on any shift of shadow or odd play of light. After five minutes of this exercise, his eyes began to blink with fatigue, but, amazingly, his hope and confidence did not dwindle. If he could just be patient, a state with which he was hardly acquainted, surely the squirrel would reveal himself when the moment was right. The moment, he realized at last, must be on the creature's terms, not his. His job was to be awake, aware, and waiting.

CHAPTER 10
A HIDDEN PATH

Davy was thinking it was time to rejoin the others when they appeared around the corner, seemingly refreshed and ready for the next leg of their hike. Anna had hung onto Mary much longer than he had predicted, but the doll was now tucked into a pocket on Jim's camera bag, its cloth head with button eyes and constant smile bobbing up and down with every step.

"Well, Davy, how far ahead did you go?" Jim asked.

"Not too far," he replied, which was the truth as he hadn't walked more than thirty paces.

"Why don't you lead for a while," Jim suggested to him. "I'll take your spot in the back."

Davy beamed.

"Why can't I go first?" Anna protested.

"How about we let you lead on the way back?" Mom offered.

"Oh, okay, I guess," she grumbled.

"It's about a quarter-mile from here to the lake," noted Jim. "I think that's enough of a destination for today. Davy, keep your eyes peeled for where the lake trail opens on your right. It's a much narrower path than this and can be easily missed."

"I won't miss it," Davy answered confidently.

"Then, let's go," said Jim, and the four were off once again.

Being in the lead meant watching his steps more carefully than ever and sounding the warning to the others if there was a log to be climbed over or a particularly rocky place to be negotiated. The trail, which until now had been fairly level, began to rise gradually as it wound up the wooded hillside. Their pace slowed, and Davy felt his pack growing heavier with every step. He encouraged himself with the thought that it would be much lighter after they ate lunch and all this uphill trudging now would be downhill cruising on the return trip. Although it was more difficult to do than ever, Davy glanced around at the towering trees when he could and kept his ears tuned to any telltale rustle in the leaves. He saw nothing and heard only the chatter of Anna's questions about what kind of flowers these were and what type of tree that was with either the answers or the occasional "I don't know" coming from Mom or Jim.

It didn't surprise him that Jim knew what so many of the plants were as he had spent most of his childhood here, but Davy was amazed at how many Mom could identify. Where had she learned all this and why had she never shared the knowledge with him on their many visits to parks or gardens in Atlanta? As he listened to Mom's responses to Anna, forgotten memories, long-buried, raced through his mind with an unbridled intensity. Yes, she had pointed out different plants during their walks but Davy, preoccupied and disinterested, had simply ignored her. Sharp pangs of guilt and remorse coursed through him. How much had he missed in the past because of his selfishness, his self-centeredness? Had Mom been hurt by or disappointed in his indifference? Why now, just as his sister, did he want to ask the questions and sincerely hear the answers? Was this new-found curiosity linked somehow to the inexplicable, overnight disappearance of his anger?

Davy relished this sense of newness and peace within him. It was like he felt on the outside after a hot, refreshing shower, clean and revived, but this was on the inside. He still couldn't explain it, but it was beginning to matter less and less whether he understood this transformation or not. The reality was that he felt more alive than he could ever remember in his life.

Everything around him took on a peculiar vibrancy of color, light and sound. He was noticing things which had never claimed his attention before. He knew he belonged to everything around him and that, somehow, it belonged to him, dwelt within him. Davy was certain that, after tasting such joy, he could never revert back to the unhappy, hateful boy he realized all too clearly he had been for far too long. To do so would be like choosing to live in a dark, dreary dungeon, clasped in chains, each link forged by his own dark, disparaging thoughts or words. *Please, God, let me stay in the light!* Davy pleaded silently, squeezing his eyes shut for a brief moment. When he opened them, there, not ten steps away from him, in the middle of the path, sat the squirrel, and not just any squirrel, indeed. This one was twice as big as any Davy had ever seen at home. The boy froze in his tracks, his mouth agape and his eyes agog. The squirrel didn't speak, but there was a friendly twinkle in his eyes and his bushy tail flicked and flailed with glee. The squirrel placed one paw at his mouth, signaling Davy to be quiet for now; with the other, he pointed to a narrow opening in the brush beside the trail to what Davy knew must be the path to the lake. Then, motioning the boy to follow, the squirrel sprang soundlessly down the trail Davy had been asked to look for. If it hadn't been for the creature's help, he felt sure, observing the entrance almost completely hidden from a casual view, that he would have missed it.

"Here's the way to the lake!" Davy shouted. He wanted to add, "I found it," but it was not the truth. The family had lagged behind him quite a distance. Knowing his new friend was already bounding away, the wait Davy endured while they caught up to him seemed interminable. When at last they were all reunited, Jim congratulated Davy on his strong scouting sense.

"Don't think I would have noticed it at all unless I knew these woods like the back of my hand. Good work, son." Jim patted Davy's shoulder good-naturedly. Like a renegade rain cloud, separated from the storm that spawned it, yet determined to challenge the sun, Davy felt a passing shadow in his heart at the word "son." In the past, he had cringed every time Jim called him that, despising the familiarity it reflected when Jim wasn't his real father. The cloud passed as rapidly as it had come, much to Davy's relief. When he gave Jim a genuine smile, he could tell that his family was relieved as well.

"C'mon, what are we waiting for?" he said, and plunged headlong down the path that would lead him to the beginning of adventures he could never have imagined.

As heavy as Davy's pack was, it was all he could do to keep from running down the trail after his new friend who, still reminding him occasionally that silence was needed for now, bounded and cavorted far ahead, but always in view as his guide. Watching the squirrel's antics tempted laughter in the worst way, but Davy managed to suppress this, knowing such behavior would confuse, if not alarm, the family. The last thing he needed, piled atop the puzzling change in his demeanor, would be for them to suppose he had utterly lost his senses. Quite the contrary; his senses had never been so keen, so discerning. To quell the urge to laugh aloud, he concentrated on the squirrel's physical appearance. Its defining color was grey, but there were hints of black and orange and silver in the fringe of the tail. The chest and torso were a creamy white as were the whiskers that stood out pertly from either side of its tawny muzzle. The ears, upright and at attention like soldiers on parade, were mostly grey with the faintest tint of orange, particularly on the tips. The nails on the strong and nimble paws were ebony black, and the rippling muscles in the haunches explained why the squirrel could accomplish such astounding leaps. Its eyes, coal-black and sparkling with intelligence and wit, were the most compelling. They met Davy's at every opportunity with openness and invitation.

"Hey, Davy, slow down!" Anna's voice rang through the forest. "We can't keep up!"

Although he had refrained from running, Davy must have been taking monumental strides as he could not bear to let the squirrel out of his sight. Immediately upon hearing Anna's request, the squirrel curtailed its speed and even stopped for several moments. It began comically tapping one foot, crossing its front paws over its chest, and feigning a "must I wait for you" whistle. With its nose in the air and its head swaying, Davy could no longer contain himself. His hearty laugh burst forth without, to the others, seeming provocation.

"What's so funny?" Anna demanded. "What's wrong with asking you to slow down? Mary's tired."

"Sorry," Davy said, still chuckling, "I guess I'm just in a hurry to see the lake."

"But, that doesn't explain why you were laughing."

"Something just struck me as funny. Is that okay?"

"I guess," Anna said, sounding unconvinced. "Are we almost there?"

"Hear the stream, Anna? That's Big Bear Creek." Jim said. "We're not five minutes away from where we're going. We should be able to see the lake any moment now, so keep a look out."

The squirrel beckoned Davy to follow, then scurried down the path at break-neck speed.

"I call seeing it first!" Davy declared and took off running as fast as his cumbersome pack allowed.

"Not fair!" Anna's wail rang in his ears.

It may not be fair, but I can't talk to the squirrel if the others are around. Maybe that's what he had in mind when he took off like that.

When Davy arrived, sweating and breathless, at the lake's edge, there was the squirrel perched on the picnic table, tapping his wrist with mock impatience as if he wore a watch.

"What took you so long, Davy? I thought you'd never arrive."

Davy hadn't even thought about how the squirrel's voice would sound. Now, hearing it for the first time, he was surprised by its tenor pitch and its lilting quality. There wasn't a trace of a chirrup as in the chatter of normal squirrels. He found himself laughing once again, this time with delight.

"Your voice, it's so, so human."

Now it was the squirrel's turn to laugh. "You were expecting Alvin of the chipmunks' fame, perhaps?" he quipped.

"Honestly, I don't know what I expected. There wasn't much time to think about it."

"You're right there, and we don't have much time to talk now with the others so close. Oh, but, I almost forgot!"

The squirrel hopped down from the table and, in two leaps, stood right in front of Davy. Sitting up on haunches, he extended his right paw to the boy.

"My name is Grey. It's my extreme pleasure to make your acquaintance, Davy."

Hesitantly, Davy bent down and reached for the offered paw; his hand enclosed it completely and he was careful not to squeeze too hard. The fur was smooth and silky, but the black claws pricked his palm ever so slightly. Grey pumped his hand vigorously.

"Oh, this is a glorious day! A glorious day! Woo-hoo!"

Grey slipped his paw from Davy's clasp and commenced to dance a wild and frenzied jig to music playing in his head. Davy, amused and amazed, found himself dancing, too, something he had always shunned, except when at the wedding reception with Grandpa Will, as the boy thought it something too awkward for him to embrace. He was just beginning to revel in it as he had then when Grey stopped abruptly and held, once again, a cautioning paw to his lips.

"I hear them coming!" he warned, as Davy obediently halted in mid step. "Davy, remember, you can hear me, but they can't. You mustn't, whatever I say, respond out loud. Can you do that? Good! Hey, do I smell pickles in your pack? And, turkey sandwiches? Child, I am famished! Oh, no! Here they are! Figure out a way to share your lunch with me, will you? The pecans I ate this morning are long gone. I'll meet you at the picnic table. Oh, and one more thing, can you convince them to eat right away? That's a good child!"

Grey scampered to the table and Davy followed, but with measured steps so as not to reveal to his family the miraculous interaction that had taken place only seconds before. He knew how to initiate the picnic and how to please Mom: set the table with plates and napkins and arrange the food in an inviting fashion. He had only seconds to unwrap his sandwich and hand half to Grey before the family emerged from the hidden path in woods. The moment was enough. His secret was safe.

Chapter 11
The Adventure Begins

Davy set right to work laying out the picnic paraphernalia. He noticed for the first time the table's surface was uncommonly clean for one set in the wild and, he assumed, rarely used. He also thought he could detect the faint odor of wood stain as if the table had been recently treated to protect it from the elements. Maybe Jim or Mr. Fairchild had seen to this task.

"Davy, what are you doing?" Mom sounded both surprised and pleased.

"I figured everyone was as hungry as I am, so I decided to unpack the lunch."

"Here, let me help you," she said and immediately busied herself arranging everything just so as Davy knew she would.

Jim had walked the short distance from the table to the stream and was setting his camera on its tripod in order to take photos of the rushing water. Anna had retrieved Mary from the camera bag and had plopped herself down on the picnic bench.

"I'm tired," she whined.

"You'll feel better after you eat," Mom assured her. "Jim, come on. Lunch is ready!"

"Be right there," he answered, making a few last lens adjustments before joining them.

It was then Mom noticed that Davy had only half of a sandwich. "Davy, when did you have time to eat half of your sandwich?"

"Right before you got here," he said. "I told you I was hungry."

"Hungry or not, you shouldn't wolf your food like that, honey. You could get indigestion."

Jim arrived at the table, the blessing was said, and everyone ate as if breakfast had never existed. Fortunately for Grey and Davy, Mom and Jim decided to rest their plates in their laps, their backs to the table, so they could better enjoy the view of the lake as they ate. Anna was preoccupied with pretending to feed Mary and was taking no notice of her brother.

"Psssst, Davy! Hand me a pickle, will you?"

Davy took a bite out of his and stealthily handed the remainder to Grey who was right by his feet under the table. He could hear the sounds of contented munching and the smacking of little lips.

"That was delicious!" the squirrel declared. "How about another and, this time, could I have a whole one?"

Davy carefully reached for another pickle and, glancing around to make sure no one was looking, delivered it to his friend. He did not dare look under the table to observe the squirrel eating as he knew the sight would make him laugh again, and it was a risk he couldn't take. He wondered, too, if when Grey took the food from him, it was invisible to everyone else? It would indeed be shocking to see a grape or potato chip levitate for an instant and then disappear by little bites into seemingly thin air. For now, he just hoped no one dropped anything on the ground and bent down to fetch it.

"Those grapes are so sweet! Let's have another, please."

Once again, Davy obliged, thinking to himself that for a little fellow, his new friend had a humongous appetite.

Just then, Jim turned around to refill his plate.

"Hey, who ate all the pickles?" Jim was partial to pickles and there was only one left in the baggie.

Davy blushed, "Sorry." He couldn't add the "I did" because, although he had taken them, he had only consumed one bite.

"That's okay," Jim said kindly. "I know all that walking and running left you half starved. If you don't mind, though, I'll take this last one since your Mom and Anna don't care for them."

"Sure," Davy said.

Under the table, Grey cringed. He never would have requested so many pickles if he had known it would place the boy in an awkward situation. He placed a tentative paw on Davy's knee.

"Is everything going to be all right?" he asked.

Davy patted the paw to let Grey know that everything was fine.

"That's a relief!" the squirrel responded and emerged from underneath the table. "Speaking of relief, all that food has made me really thirsty. I'm going to go get a drink from the stream. There is a narrow trail that runs beside it and disappears into the woods. We can talk there and not be heard, but you will still be in earshot of your folks if they start calling for you. Tell them you want to explore along the stream and look for, oh, I don't know, rocks or something. Jim is sure to convince your mother that you'll be safe. He knows this forest almost as well as I do."

Here Grey paused. Davy noticed that the squirrel was gazing at Jim with an unfettered fondness, as a doting parent regards a precious child.

"I always wished that Jim had the gift," he spoke softly. "But, that was not something we could make happen."

Grey's eyes turned to Davy. The boy glimpsed the unmistakable trace of sadness in them and he found himself feeling truly sorry for Jim for the first time in his life.

As if sensing his thoughts, Grey said, "You have a great heart, Davy. I am looking forward to knowing it, and you, better. Hurry, now; the adventure begins!"

With that, Grey scampered off to the stream where he took several long drinks, dried his mouth with the back of his paw, then waved to Davy and pointed out the way he was to go. In a flash, the squirrel vanished into the forest's shadows.

"Davy, you've been awfully quiet at lunch."

Davy heard Mom's voice as if it were a distant murmur. His ears were full with the rush of the stream and Grey's words still echoing in his mind. Someone touched his arm and he jumped, almost falling off the picnic bench.

"Oh, honey, did I startle you?" Mom wore her worried look. "I'm so sorry. That must have been quite a daydream you were having."

Davy recovered and managed to give her a weak smile. Yes, he had been deep in thought, more in tune now with Grey's world than with the other reality that surrounded him.

Mom continued, "A penny for your thoughts?"

"More like a dollar, Kate," Jim chuckled. "Davy was on another planet."

Davy knew he had to ask about exploring along the stream and this moment was the perfect opportunity. They both wanted to know what he had been thinking. Had Grey been right in saying that Jim would be supportive of him? He wouldn't know unless he posed the question. Davy took a deep breath before he began.

"I was thinking that I would like to explore the stream, walk along it, see where it goes; I don't know, maybe collect some rocks."

"Rocks?" Mom asked incredulously. "Since when have you been interested in rock collecting?"

"Since, uh, since today?" Davy said. He knew how unconvincing this answer was and he mentally kicked himself for sounding so stupid.

Unanticipated, Jim came to his rescue. "Kate, we saw a lot of quartz on our way to the lake; beautiful stones, they are. Maybe Davy wants to try to find some of them and start a collection. It's not a bad hobby. Plus, there are some beautiful, water-worn rocks, which you can only see by the stream. Oh, and if he finds any flat ones, he can bring them back to us, so we can have a rock-skipping contest in the lake."

Davy could hardly believe his ears. Yes, he had noticed the gem-like stones on their walk, but that memory hadn't surfaced in time to bolster his argument. Now, here was Jim, a man that not twenty-four hours ago was the enemy, coming to his aid as sure as any fellow soldier.

"But, Jim," Mom protested, "Davy doesn't know these woods yet. What if he gets lost or slips and falls into the water or wanders into a patch of poison ivy?"

Jim put his arms around Mom, a gesture that Davy had previously detested, but one that was sure to calm her and allay her unfounded fears.

"Kate, I was only eight when Grandpa let me roam these woods. Davy knows to stay on the trail and, watching him gallop down the last stretch to the lake, I'd say he's as sure-footed as a mountain goat."

Mom was still not convinced.

"Tell you what," said Jim, "I'll give him my watch and we'll tell him what time he needs to return. I'll even set the alarm to remind him."

Sensing that the tide was turning in his favor, Davy interjected, "I won't go far, Mom, really, I won't. Jim can holler to me every five minutes and, if I can't hear him, I'll come back to where I can hear. Please let me go exploring on my own!"

Mom's expression was one of consternation and apprehension. She searched Jim's face, then Davy's, and, finally, returned to Jim's. This battle, Mom decided, was like the one with last night's Sprites, lost before it was even begun. She heaved a sigh as if trying to will her fears and doubts exhaled with it.

"Okay, honey," she said quietly. "As long as you have Jim's watch and you pay attention to where you are and what you are doing at all times, you can go on your adventure."

"Thanks, Mom!" Davy shouted and ran around the table to give her a hug which she reciprocated with gusto.

"Here, Davy, I've set the alarm for you," Jim smiled at him and winked. "The watch is too large for your wrist, so you'll have to keep it in your pocket. Take your pack with you so you can carry some rocks back."

Davy cradled the watch in his hand, feeling its weight before slipping it into his pocket. Then, he shouldered his almost weightless pack with a boundless joy. He vowed to himself that he would come back with some rocks and was sure that Grey would help him search for these.

"I'm going to take some pictures of the stream, so I'll see that Davy gets off on the right foot," Jim said, kissing Mom lightly on the forehead. "Don't worry, Kate. Everything is better than all right."

Now it was Mom's turn to offer a tentative smile. "If you say so," she whispered.

"Mom," Anna piped up, "can you take us wading in the lake? Mary and I are bored and we want to have some fun."

"Sure thing," said Mom, "but I think Mary might enjoy it more if she didn't get wet."

"She can get wet, Kate," Jim assured her, "she's made of cloth."

"Okay," Mom said, now smiling impishly, "and if she does get wet, I'll let you carry her home in your pocket."

"Fair enough," laughed Jim. "Let's go, Davy."

As the two walked toward the stream, they heard shrieks of surprise from Anna.

"Oh, Mom, the water is so cold!"

"Just wade in a tiny step at a time, honey, you'll get used to it."

You'll get used to it. The words echoed in Davy's ears. Embarking on this venture left him pondering about whether he would ever, could ever, get used to talking with and seeing creatures which no one else could see or hear. How would he keep the others from finding out? He had so many questions for Grey. Why could the squirrel speak perfect English? Why could he only be seen by a select few? Who and what was he in truth? Flushed with excitement and curiosity, Davy longed to know everything at once.

Tiny step at a time, honey, tiny step at a time. Your adventure is just beginning . . .

Chapter 12

True Squirrel of the Old Ones

"You've got an hour," Jim told Davy when they arrived at the creek. "That should be more than enough time to do some exploring and rock-collecting, don't you think?"

Davy knew that an eternity wouldn't be enough time to spend with Grey, but he gave Jim a nod in the affirmative and felt to make sure that the watch was still secured in his pocket.

"There's the trail," Jim said, pointing. "It's a bit tricky in some spots, so watch your step. You don't want to end up in the creek and have to hike home in wet clothes."

"No, sir," Davy answered.

Jim grinned broadly at the boy and patted his shoulder. "Better get along then."

Davy turned and started up the trail. After several steps, he stopped and looked behind him. Jim was already bent over his camera. He could just glimpse Mom and Anna still wading in the lake. It suddenly dawned on him that he would be in the lake, too, had his step-father not intervened on his behalf.

"Hey, Jim?" he called.

Jim glanced up at him where he stood half-hidden in the dappled shade.

"Thanks!" he said sincerely.

Jim smiled and gave him two thumbs up.

Davy returned the smile, waved, and headed up the trail as rapidly as he dared after Jim's warning. Although the woods had been shady and cool during his hike with the family, now walking alongside Big Bear Creek, it felt just like air-conditioning. Davy inhaled deeply, refreshed anew with each breath. The path bent to the right, following the stream, becoming rougher with each step. Large boulders, most adorned with lush moss, were scattered from the path to the creek bed as if ancient giants had engaged in a game of shot put. Davy had to negotiate these carefully, many times using both hands to hoist himself up onto them to keep moving forward or grasping the support of roots and slender tree trunks to help him detour the obstacles.

The lake was now completely hidden from view, and he couldn't hear anything except the ceaseless babbling of the creek. Just how far could Grey have gone? Davy thought that this location was sequestered enough for their meeting, but perhaps his friend knew of a more reclusive and safer place. He trudged on, painfully conscious of how the time he would be able to share freely with Grey was slipping away with every second that passed.

Just as worried thoughts began seeping into his mind, a cheerful voice promptly washed them away.

"Davy! Up here!"

Davy's eyes scanned the sloping embankment. There, perched on a flat slab of rock was a camouflaged Grey, his tail and whiskers twitching; his sharp eyes were bright and shiny, giving his position away. Davy clambered up the hillside as fast as he could and within seconds was seated beside the squirrel on the smooth stone which made a perfect bench for two. The mad scramble left him rather breathless, and it took him several moments before he could speak.

"Why did you go so far along the trail?" he asked.

"To get to this comfortable seat, of course," Grey answered. "I guess I momentarily forgot how slowly you humans move, especially along a rocky trail. I actually began to wonder if you were going to make it and was about to go looking for you, when, there you were."

"Yes," Davy smiled gratefully. "Here I am, and I'm talking to a squirrel, or," and here he paused, studying his friend from head to toe, "is a squirrel what you really are?"

"Dear child!" Grey feigned indignation and placed his right paw over his heart. "What stands here before your eyes is a True Squirrel of the Old Ones from the Beginning!"

Here, Grey pulled himself to his full height so that he could look Davy squarely in the face. His expression was solemn, indeed reverent, and his eyes closed briefly as if recalling a fleeting prayer. When he opened them, they were twinkling.

"And you know nothing of us, do you, Davy?"

"No," he answered, "but, you'll tell me more, won't you?"

Hearing the eagerness in the boy's voice thrilled Grey. How many years had it been since he had ushered the young Will into the world of the Old Ones by answering his many questions? He hadn't had the need to tell the story once Will had heard it because there was no one else to share it with. This was an opportunity to savor; Grey would share it all with Davy, but not all at once. His whiskers quivered with anticipation.

"Yes, Davy," he said. "You will know all about the Old Ones. However, learning about us a bit at a time might be best."

Davy thought about having to take it one step at a time. Seeing a look of disappointment cloud the boy's face, Grey hastily added, "That way, each day we are together this summer will answer a fresh question. You'll always have something to look forward to when you see me."

"But, just seeing you and talking to you are reasons enough for me," Davy insisted.

Grey found himself unexpectedly touched by the boy's words and his eyes brimmed with tears that he briskly brushed away with the back of a paw. He leaned over to give Davy's hand a reassuring pat.

"And those are reasons enough for me as well, child," he said. "But, being practical, we haven't much time left today and, if I began the story now, I would have to rush and would certainly leave out important details. We wouldn't want that, now, would we?"

"No, I guess not," Davy replied, "but, will you answer at least one of my questions today?"

"I don't see why not, as long as it is one I can answer," said Grey. "However, to be fair, I have to ask you a question, too. Although your great-grandpa told me some things about you, there is much that I, too, need to learn about you, my young friend."

"That's fine," Davy agreed, smiling again to hear the squirrel call him "friend." "Who goes first?"

"We'll do rock-paper-scissors to decide," said Grey.

"You know about that?" Davy's eyes grew wide with incredulity.

"Know about it? The game was invented by the Old Ones, the raccoons to be exact. Clever paws, they have, don't you agree?"

Davy said he did but, secretly, wondered in what way they were "clever." How he wished he had read more about animals or at least watched Animal Planet!

"Okay, ready? Here we go!" said Grey. They counted to three together, Davy tickled by seeing the squirrel pound one open paw with the other that was balled up as best it could be to resemble a fist. In a split second, he knew that paper would be easiest for Grey and decided to do scissors. The squirrel trumped him, keeping his paw exactly like it was when they were counting.

"Ah, ha!" Grey exclaimed delightedly. "It looks like I'll be going first."

Davy knew his friend had won fair and square, but he couldn't help feeling a bit let down. Grey noticed immediately.

"Cheer up, Davy. After all, I've already told you something about the Old Ones that you didn't know, so you actually get at least two today."

"You're right," he admitted, giving Grey a crooked grin. "Okay, Grey, what do you want to ask me?"

"Let's see," said the squirrel, posing one paw under his furry chin, his brow furrowed in thought. "What's a good first question for you?"

Grey tapped one foot as if keeping in time with an internal tune.

"I've got it!" He announced abruptly. "Davy, how do you like having Jim as a stepfather?"

The question stunned Davy. He had expected something more along the lines of "What are your favorite games?" or "What are your favorite foods?" The latter was particularly relevant in light of Grey's seemingly enormous appetite, but this? Davy's mind raced through the numerous incidences in the past where he had been intentionally rude to Jim, resenting his very presence in his family's lives, and how now, literally overnight, the relationship had experienced a dramatic change for the better.

He knew that Grey was fond of Jim and he dreaded telling his new friend how horrible he had acted toward the man before today. Yet, when he lifted his head and met Grey's gaze, so steady and patient, he knew he could do nothing other than tell the truth. Heaving a heart-felt sigh, Davy plunged in, but not without a prayer that his friend would still be his friend when he finished.

Grey listened without judgment or interruption as Davy recounted how Jim had come into their lives and how he had disliked him from the outset. After he married Mom, it seemed that everything went from bad to worse, and the decision to force him to spend his summer at some remote farm was the straw that broke the camel's back.

"The last place I thought I wanted to spend the summer was here, without a television, a computer, or a swimming pool. I was angrier with Jim than ever for making us come, and I couldn't let go of those bad feelings about him. Then, this morning when I woke up, the anger was gone, vanished, just like that!"

Davy snapped his fingers for emphasis. Grey nodded and smiled mysteriously, already knowing that part of the story, but Davy ignored this for the moment and continued on.

"I don't know what happened to me and I don't know why, but today, for the first time in forever, I feel like the self I'm supposed to be, though I can't be sure that I even understand that self. The one thing I DO know is that I never want to be the old Davy again."

"Oh, you'll have your moments here and there," Grey advised him, "but, no, you will never slip back completely into your old and, may I say frankly, rather regrettable ways."

"How can you be so sure?" Davy wondered.

"Because," said Grey solemnly, "you have received the blessing of Wise One."

An inexplicable yet delicious thrill coursed through Davy's veins as if the words Grey had just spoken were blessing him all over again. He closed his eyes and shivered involuntarily. It was not a chilling, teeth-chattering shiver, but one that arose from an intensity of warmth within him. He felt as though he had swallowed a beam of sunshine and its light was radiating throughout every inch of his body. Then, without Grey having to say a word, Davy understood fully what had transpired the night before.

"That's why I fell asleep so quickly last night!" he exclaimed. He groped in his pocket for the bird feather he had forgotten about until this moment. He held it up for Grey to see.

"This feather was under my bed this morning. It belongs to the owl you call Wise One!" Davy didn't know how he knew with such certainty that it was an owl's feather, but he didn't pause to question.

"Yes, it does," Grey said with a chuckle, "and he was not too keen on parting with it. But, it couldn't be helped, I told him, seeing as I needed something to wipe off your PSP screen."

"So, you're the one who turned it off and left it on the table for me," Davy said and, after perusing the squirrel's stature afresh, added, "that couldn't have been easy for you unless, of course, the Old Ones have super strength."

This thought amused Grey, and he laughed out loud, "There are many gifts that were granted to the Old Ones, child, but superior physical strength wasn't one of them. Yes, moving your toy was quite a struggle, especially since I had gotten too deep a whiff of the sleep prayer, but I managed it, and now you've managed to have a question answered without really asking it."

Davy slapped his hand to his forehead and grimaced. He desperately wanted to know what gifts Grey had, but it was no longer his turn to ask. Sensing the boy's frustration and knowing that he was near to bursting from curiosity, Grey patted his shoulder comfortingly. Davy was immediately calmed.

"Thank you, Grey, for taking care of my PSP," he said softly. "If you hadn't, I would have dead batteries right now."

"Don't mention it," the squirrel said kindly. "It's a joy to do something kind for a friend but, remember," said the squirrel, pointing what humans would call the index finger of his paw and fixing Davy's gaze to his own, "it's doubly joyful to show kindness toward someone you don't like, for instance, Jim."

Before Davy could wrap his mind around this last statement, the alarm on Jim's watch shattered the stillness.

"Oh, no!" Davy cried out in dismay. "I forgot to check the time and now I'm going to be late getting back to the lake!"

"Not if I can help it," Grey smiled. "Give me your hands."

Davy didn't see how that would solve his predicament, but he did as Grey requested. The squirrel laid his front paws in Davy's outstretched palms and the boy's fingers folded gently over them.

"Now, my child, close your eyes and, whatever you do, don't open them until I say to."

Grey then spoke the following words:

> *Speed of angels, speed of light,*
> *Swiftly take us both in flight*
> *Away from here and on to where*
> *My mind envisions, bring us there.*

A roaring wind filled Davy's ears and rainbow colors danced on the surface of his tightly closed eyelids. For a brief second, his body seemed weightless, and he imagined himself a white, billowing cloud floating in a carefree blue sky. Then, as instantly as it had begun, the wind died and he was aware of his legs standing firmly on solid ground.

"You may open your eyes now," Grey told him, his voice barely audible after the rush of wind that left his ears ringing with its echo.

Davy opened his eyes and blinked with astonishment. He was standing with Grey at the beginning of the trail beside Big Bear Creek. There was Jim, just packing up his camera gear. Mom and Anna were tidying up the picnic table and preparing for the trek back to the house.

"You need to close your mouth before you catch a fly," Grey chortled.

It was then Davy realized that his whole face exuded his amazement at the feat just performed. Adjusting his expression accordingly, he gradually released the squirrel's rather squished paws from his vise-like grip. Grey rubbed them together, as he said, to encourage the return of circulation.

"And that, my child, answers another question not asked, does it not?" he said with a smile. Davy nodded silently, still reeling from their miraculous journey.

Just then, Jim looked up and saw Davy standing on the trail. "Hey there, you're right on time, son. Way to go! Did you find many rocks?"

Davy was instantly panic-stricken. In his desire to spend every possible moment with Grey, he had completely forgotten about collecting rocks. His eyes turned a mute plea on the squirrel.

"Get ready," he warned, "your pack is about to gain some weight!"

Thump! Davy almost staggered under the sudden load, but managed to keep his footing.

"Yes," he called to Jim, "I have some. I'll show you when we get home."

"Thanks," Davy whispered to Grey who had once again come to his rescue.

"Anytime," said the squirrel, "and, by the way, if you're wondering why I couldn't pull that trick with your PSP, it's because it's not made from natural materials. It's a bit inconvenient in this day and time what with all your man-made implements, but changing times do not change the Gifts."

"Jim! We're ready to go. Where's Davy?" Mom's voice rang clearly above the gurgling stream.

"I'm here, Mom," he shouted back.

"You best get going," said Grey, "before they start wondering why you are standing here like a statue. I have some business that I must tend to for the moment."

Davy was crestfallen, and he knew the disappointment showed in his face.

"Don't fret; child, I'll see you again before you know it."

With that, the True Squirrel of the Old Ones leaped onto Davy's shoulder and, planting a whiskery kiss on the top of his head, scampered up the nearest tree trunk and vanished into the branches.

CHAPTER 13
A TERRIFYING TURN

The hike back to the house that afternoon seemed longer to Davy than it had that morning, even with the more frequent downhill sequences. His pack, weighted as it was by the unknown stones, felt heavier than it had when he toted the picnic lunch and the muscles in his legs and back were beginning to ache. Anna had whined her way to a piggyback ride from Jim which left Mom to carry the camera equipment as well as her own small pack and binoculars. Davy had offered to help with Mom's load, but she insisted she was fine.

"Besides, honey, you gathered all those rocks. You don't need to be carrying anything else. I'm just so proud of you for being responsible on your own along the trail and returning when we asked you to."

Davy felt a flush of guilt rise to his face already crimson with the heat of exertion. If it hadn't been for Grey's miraculous intervention, he would have been at least ten minutes late in arriving at the lake, an inconvenience for his waiting family and irrefutable proof that he could not be trusted to follow through with the simplest of requests. As he could not share the truth with Mom unless he wished to betray Grey's presence, he vowed then and there to keep track of the time in any future expeditions he undertook.

That would not be easy since he had always been a child who needed prodding to stay on schedule, whether it was to get up for school, catch the school bus, or remember when a project was due, but Davy was determined to alter his former ways. *After all, he thought, the "old" me is gone, so maybe some of my bad habits disappeared with that old me, too.*

Inspired by this thought, he took a deep breath and, upon exhaling, envisioned the last remnants of his former self departing from him, dissipating in the welcome breeze that soothed his sweaty forehead. Davy wiped his brow with the tail of this T-shirt and began to pay more attention to the forest around him than the path as it had now smoothed out considerably. How he longed to see Grey frolicking in the limbs above him! Why the squirrel had to leave him just as they were getting acquainted was a mystery. Surely, it must have been something of utmost importance and urgency, but what that could possibly be, Davy had no clue. Whatever it was, he fervently hoped that it would not keep him separated from his new and marvelous friend for long.

As he walked, Davy let his thoughts meander through the day's remarkable events. He knew that in light of their fantastic nature, he should either be overwhelmed with awe or be seriously questioning the stability of his senses, but he was neither. Instead, he basked in the certainty that he had experienced a truer reality than he could have ever imagined. Grey was a living, breathing soul, as tangible as the leaves which fluttered above him, as approachable as his own family. *But, what kind of soul? Who were the Old Ones and what had the squirrel meant by "the Beginning?" The beginning of what? Of the earth? Of time? Of the mountains that defined this place? Could it be that the Old Ones were immortal?*

Innumerable questions buzzed in Davy's head like a persistent swarm of bees. He longed for the answers that would quiet them, but none would be forthcoming until Grey returned. With great effort, he pushed the queries to the back of his mind and set his focus on the trail and his new home that could not be much farther away.

Davy pictured his special room on the screened porch and tried to recall each picture and item that had been thoughtfully placed there just for him. It was then that the image of Maggie, snoring gently on her bed at the foot of his, popped into view. His desire to reach the house to be with her imparted a fresh resolve to his tired muscles. He could hardly wait to hug her neck and bury his face in her soft fur. Davy felt a twinge of guilt. For most of this outing, he really hadn't thought of the first creature who befriended him upon his arrival here; he had been too enthralled by Grey.

But now, as he could glimpse the end of the path where it exited the woods and led to the farmhouse, his eagerness to be reunited with the dog filled his thoughts to the exclusion, thankfully, for the time being, of all the others for which answers could not be found. The only question floating through his mind now was if Maggie had missed him. Would she waggle her tail in greeting? Would she lick his face and lean against him in an invitation to scratch her back? Would she rest her chin on his leg while they ate as she had the night before? He would know in only a matter of moments. Suddenly, Davy's ears caught the faint sound of Maggie's excited barking. *She must sense me coming home,* Davy thought gleefully, his face beaming.

"Down we get, Miss Priss," Jim said to Anna as they emerged from the forest's shade into the brightness of the afternoon sun. "I think your legs can make it to the house on their own now.

"Race ya!" Davy shouted to his sister and burst out of the forest with such speed that even Mom was amazed.

"Not fair!" Anna's predictable protest rang out. "I'm tired!"

"Where does he get all that energy, I wonder?" Mom said to Jim as she came alongside him.

"I'd say he's just a typical, growing boy, Kate. Did you notice how much he ate at lunch today?" Jim asked as he put his arm around her. "He's hurrying all for nothing, though, because the door is locked."

Jim took the camera bag from her and a wince of pain flashed momentarily across his face.

"Honey, are you all right?" Kate asked, her voice tinged with fear.

"Just my back acting up a little," Jim admitted and smiled sheepishly. "I guess I should have listened to you when you cautioned me against carrying Anna such a long way. She's definitely not as small as she used to be."

Both of them watched as Davy reached the porch steps full tilt and Anna, pigtails flying and Mary in tow, sprinted with everything she had even though she realized her brother would beat her.

"Thanks to you," Kate said, "she has energy to spare, but," and here she feigned a scolding, "you are headed for a hot bath and a heating pad. The last thing you need now is for your back to give out."

"Yes, dear," Jim said with a subservient air.

"Oh, stop that!" Kate giggled. "I'm only trying to help."

Jim laughed and wrapped his arms around her. "Don't you think I know that? You take such good care of this old man."

"And, stop that, too," she insisted. "I don't call forty-one old, and neither should you."

Jim was just about to tease her with another "yes, dear" but stopped dead in his tracks. A serious pall enveloped his face and the trepidation in his eyes was palpable. Startled, Kate followed his gaze just in time to see Davy backing slowly down the porch steps, Anna's hand in his, and Maggie, tail wagging like a flag at a Fourth of July parade, close at his side.

"I thought you said you locked it?" she whispered.

Jim thrust a hand into his pocket and produced a humongous key ring.

"I KNOW I locked it," he declared and grabbed her hand as he broke into a breathless sprint for the children who had turned and were running toward them. Davy and Anna flew into Mom's arms.

"The door," Davy panted. "Someone unlocked it, left it open."

"Surely, it must be that the Fairchilds stopped by," said Mom with a forced optimism.

"Honey, I hate to tell you this, but Bob and Susie never let themselves in without asking, and they'd never leave the door unlocked while there."

Kate could tell Jim's voice was barely under control, and saw her children's eyes darting worriedly from one adult face to the other, seeking solace in this terrifying turn of events.

"Kate," Jim said with a firm calmness, "walk with the kids down to the Fairchild's house. You know where it is. Be sure to keep the dog with you. Stay there until I call or come for you."

Kate's legs felt like lead and her body trembled all over. She couldn't move.

"Davy," Jim saluted, "take your Mom's and sister's hands and do as I've asked."

"Yes, sir," said Davy with a braveness he certainly didn't feel.

"You reacted like a soldier, son, when you saw the door open; you protected your sister. I trust you'll guide your mom and her to safety."

Jim tousled Davy's hair gently, yet the boy could sense a precarious tension in the touch.

"Go, now, and quickly," Jim ordered them, his voice not more than a whisper.

Daring not to hesitate, Davy propelled his mother and sister into action. Maggie, grateful to be reunited with her new family, trotted unusually briskly a few paces ahead of them as they hastened down the gravel road to the Fairchild's cabin. No one spoke, but Davy couldn't help noticing the stream of tears coursing down his mother's cheeks. His heart rose to his throat and he found himself choking back his own unbidden sobs. Anna clutched Mary tenaciously to her chest, and though her eyes were dry, her expression was one of unbridled fear.

As fatigued as they were, the three never slowed nor faltered until the welcome sight of the Fairchild's pickup truck parked comfortingly by their cabin was in view. It was then, as if in one accord, they broke into a run. Maggie barked enthusiastically at the sudden increase of pace as if she was worried that she couldn't keep up with them. Her herald beckoned Bob Fairchild to his front door before they even reached the steps.

"Kate! Kids! What's wrong? Where's Jim?" Bob cried out in alarm as he hurried to meet them.

Just then, two gun shots rang out, disproportionately magnified as they echoed against the surrounding mountain sides. Uttering a cry of anguish, Kate collapsed to the ground.

WHAT HAS HAPPENED TO KATE?
IS SHE GOING TO BE ALL RIGHT?
AND, WHAT ABOUT DAVY AND GREY?
WILL THERE BE MORE ADVENTURES?

You'll find all the answers in Book 2 of
The Glade series entitled *Children in the
Garden*. Look for it online and at local
bookstores in early 2013.

ABOUT THE AUTHOR

Martha Jane Orlando fell in love with the Nantahala Mountains of North Carolina when her husband, Danny, and she stayed there on their honeymoon. The majestic scenery, sparkling streams, and wooded trails create the perfect backdrop for her trilogy, *The Glade*.

Martha Jane is a former middle school teacher who has a son and a daughter, and two stepsons, all grown. She is well acquainted with the challenges and joys of a blended family, and many of the situations described in *A Trip, a Tryst and a Terror* mirror her own personal experiences.

Aside from writing fiction, Martha Jane also pens a bi-weekly devotional blog, *Meditations of my Heart*, which you can visit at marthaorlando.blogspot.com. She has created a fan page for *The Glade* which you can visit at gladetrilogy.wix.com/theglade. Your comments and feedback are warmly welcomed!

Martha Jane will be the first to tell you that her passion for writing runs second only to her passionate love for the Lord. She is blessed to help Danny lead contemporary worship each Sunday at their church, Kennesaw United Methodist, in Kennesaw, Georgia, where she resides.

CPSIA information can be obtained at www.ICGtesting.com
Printed in the USA
BVOW070850191212

308678BV00001B/71/P